A LITTLE LOVING

Annabel's attention was caught by a young man standing over by the stereo on the other side of the room. He had dark blond hair, a light suntan, high cheekbones, and a mouth like a sulky angel. Annabel stared.

'Who's that, Jacqui?'

'Who?'

'The guy in the blue jumper, over there.'

Jacqui looked. 'Oh, I keep forgetting you two haven't met. That's Richard, Ben's new assistant!'

Annabel looked again. It wasn't, she decided, his undoubted good looks that made her look twice at him. The room was full of handsome men. This Richard seemed something of an outsider. He wasn't talking to anyone, he wasn't dancing, he wasn't drinking. He was simply . . . observing. Annabel was intrigued.

'What's he like, Jacqui? As a person, I mean?'

Jacqui frowned. 'Difficult to say. He's not an easy guy to get close to. Annie, you're blushing!'

And suddenly Richard was beside them . . .

A LITTLE LOVING

JILL ECKERSLEY

A Sapphire Romance

Hamlyn Paperbacks

A LITTLE LOVING
ISBN 0 600 20154 6

First published in Great Britain 1981
by Hamlyn Paperbacks
Copyright © 1981 by Jill Eckersley

Hamlyn Paperbacks are published by
The Hamlyn Publishing Group Ltd,
Astronaut House,
Feltham, Middlesex, England
(Paperback Division: Hamlyn Paperbacks,
Banda House, Cambridge Grove,
Hammersmith, London W6 0LE)

Printed and bound in Great Britain by
©ollins, Glasgow

*For Ray, and the Lions —
with love and exasperation!*

I

Annabel was late, and there was a traffic jam at Baker Street, as usual. She tapped her foot impatiently as she waited for the green light, ignoring the appreciative comments of the taxi driver who had pulled up beside her. The lights changed and the MGB crawled forward, but the traffic was too snarled-up to let her through and she was forced to pull up again ten yards farther on.

That'll teach me to stay up half the night nattering with Cindi, she thought ruefully, peering at herself in the driving mirror. She hadn't had time to put any make-up on, and her long auburn hair was hastily pinned up under a gold silk scarf. I look a wreck, she thought dispassionately. Thank heavens I'm not modelling any more. There are times when it's an advantage not to have to try to look stunning all the time...

The lights changed at last and the white MGB surged forward and on to Marylebone Road. The snubbed driver got his own back by cutting in in front of her and forcing her to slow down. Idiot, she thought, glaring at him. I'll never get to work at this rate! Imperceptibly, as she headed towards the Westway flyover, she put her foot down.

At the narrow turning into Lauriston Mews she braked sharply, and the MGB's tyres squealed in protest. She parked hastily and got out, fumbling in her handbag for her keys. Even on a morning like this her spirits lifted when she saw the smart, white-painted front door with ANNABEL LEE, MODEL AGENCY picked out in green and gold. She ran up the stairs two at a time, called 'Morning, Gillian!' to the receptionist, and collapsed into her own chair.

'Suzy, could you –'

Before she had time to say another word, a mug of black coffee had appeared on her desk. She sipped it gratefully. 'Suzy, you're an angel. I'm so sorry I'm late. When's that American girl coming in?' Suzy, her assistant, smiled at her. 'Relax, Annie, there's no rush. She called me half an hour ago to say that she was still very jet-lagged and could she come and see us this afternoon instead. I said that was fine.'

Annabel heaved a sigh of relief. 'Thank goodness for that! I knew she was coming in at ten-thirty, and I just couldn't get anywhere this morning. I overslept anyway, and then I got stuck in the traffic and some stupid cab driver did his best to cut me up. Honestly, there are some men who make a point of playing boy-racers as soon as they see a girl in a sports car! Anything else come up?'

'No, nothing serious. Everyone seems to be OK this morning, touch wood!'

At last Annabel relaxed and smiled at Suzy, her right-hand girl, thinking, not for the first time, how lucky she was to have found her. Meticulous, unflappable Suzy was the girl who would check and double-check bookings, get every agreement in writing, type letters, count and file invoices, arrange photo-sessions, mother shy new models and temperamental photographers, and generally help the Annabel Lee Agency to continue to be the efficient operation that it was.

'Ben phoned,' said Suzy. 'He said he's going to pop in this afternoon because he's got some new photos of Jacqui and the children he wants to show us.'

'Bless him!' said Annabel.

Ben and Jacqui Lawrence were her best friends. Jacqui was also one of the agency's most successful models, even though at twenty-six, two years older than Annabel, she was at the age when a lot of models are thinking about retiring. Jacqui Lawrence, whose perfect bone structure and smooth fair hair reminded everyone she met of Grace Kelly, had taken Annabel under her wing when she first came to London as an ambitious seventeen-year-old. Armed with nothing more than red hair, long legs, and a lot of determination, Annabel had her sights set on making it as a top model. It hadn't taken her very long to realize that nearly every other skinny provincial redhead had the same idea, not to mention the blondes and the brunettes. Annabel's first agency had done next to nothing for her apart from introducing her to Jacqui, already a rising star, and the two girls had been fast friends from then on. Jacqui had been luckier than Annabel in two respects. For one thing, her naturally serene personality made her an easy model to work with. Secondly, just before she met Annabel she had married Ben Lawrence, whose reputation as one of the best fashion photographers in London was already established.

Jacqui loved modelling, but Annabel found she hated it. She hated trying to sell her face and figure to the right people; she was too proud to enjoy being pushed around by surly photographers who considered themselves creative artists and models less than nothing. She hated the endless round of interviews and auditions with indifferent fashion editors who flipped through her model book in thirty seconds and handed it back without even looking at her. Castings for commercials were worse; being ordered to stand, sit, walk, run, jump or smile for a bunch of cold-eyed, overweight film-makers who looked at her 'like horse-traders at a country fair!' as she complained indignantly to Jacqui. But Jacqui had only shrugged and smiled her beautiful gentle smile and said, 'But that's the job, honey, that's what it's all about. What did you think it would be like?'

'Not like this!' Annabel had cried.

What *had* she thought, trapped in the poky, ill-furnished terraced house in Nottingham with her gentle shadow of a mother? She had thought that there had to be more to life than the secretarial course the teachers at school were trying to push her into, more than the drab red-brick streets where children kicked tin cans along the pavements and fat old women in print aprons gossiped in their open doorways. Somewhere, there was a world where girls were slim and beautiful and clothes were soft and swirling and expensive and cars were sleek and powerful and men were reckless and charming. Anne Lee from Nottingham intended to be part of that world, somehow.

'Anne Lee?' she remembered her first agent saying. 'Darling, you need something a bit more memorable than that! How about ... let me see ... Anna? Annette? Anji? Anji Lee, how does that sound?'

'Annabel Lee sounds better.'

'Annabel ... Lee. Mmmm. It sounds familiar. Are you sure there isn't another model with that name?'

'It's a poem,' she had said witheringly. 'It's a poem by Edgar Allan Poe. I did it as part of my English A level.'

'Really?' the agent replied, uninterested. 'OK dear, Annabel Lee it is.'

Suzy's voice brought Annabel back to the present. 'How come you're so tired today, Annie? Did you have a heavy night?'

Annabel grinned. 'In a way. Cindi got in about three after doing a night flight from Dallas. She brought a bottle of wine and we sat up drinking it and nattering, and the next thing we knew it was daylight, and we were both feeling like death on legs! Of course it's all right for her, she's got a couple of days off, so she crawled off to bed and I washed my hair, but I fell asleep while it was drying, and didn't wake up again till nearly ten o'clock.'

'You and Cindi are like a couple of schoolkids when you get together.'

'I suppose we are!'

Cindi Charlesworth, who shared Annabel's Primrose Hill flat, was an American air stewardess whose exploits with infatuated passengers kept Annabel entertained for hours.

'Go on, who is it this time?' teased Suzy, who had heard all about Cindi's romances with, in turn, an Indian doctor, an Arab oil millionaire, a French racing driver and about four pilots, each more extraordinary than the last.

'It's a Texan rancher, would you believe,' said Annabel. 'He was so keen to get her over to his ranch that he ended up inviting the entire crew to spend all their free time there! Cindi said it was absolutely fantastic, with indoor and outdoor pools, saunas, floodlit tennis courts, Lord knows how many horses and everything!'

'Why don't I ever meet anyone like that?' Suzy said enviously.

'Well, I don't, either. Maybe you have to be an air stewardess!' joked Annabel.

'Ah, but you've got Leonard, Annie!'

Annabel smiled. 'True. I mustn't be greedy, must I?'

What more could anyone want than someone like Leonard, Annabel thought to herself. Kind, intelligent, rich – and devoted to me. The answer to any girl's prayer, but especially mine. It was Leonard who had appeared out of the blue, almost three years previously, and solved all Annabel's problems at once. An old friend of her late father's, he had agreed to finance her new and very private dream, of running her own model agency. Annabel could never remember when the idea had first occurred to her, but it had been some time between her earliest modelling jobs and Leonard's getting in touch with her. She could remember confiding in Jacqui after yet another row with their agent who had complained, with some justification, that if Annabel intended to go on being sulky and unco-operative, she might as well give up the idea of being a model altogether.

'One day, Jacqui, I'll have my own agency,' she had said.

'Why don't you?' said Jacqui sympathetically. 'You're wasted as a model, Annie. You'd be much happier with your own business!'

'But I can't afford it!' Annabel complained. 'I need a

backer, and there just isn't anyone. My mother can't help ...
there's no one, unless I save enough out of what I earn, and
if I keep storming out of sessions like I did today I'll never
make any money!'

And then, Leonard. Leonard, who had agreed to finance
the Annabel Lee Agency in return for the privilege of taking
out the beautiful Annabel Lee, someone he could pet and
indulge as he did his beloved Siamese cat. Annabel's face
softened as she thought of him. Dear Leonard, always there,
always comforting, always on her side, a cross between the
father she barely remembered and a very special friend;
Leonard who had smoothed away the scars of her first,
desperately unhappy love-affair with one of the reckless and
charming playboys she had longed to meet in those far-off
days in Nottingham ...

Annabel and Suzy had just finished their lunch when Ben
Lawrence poked his head round the office door and smiled at
them. 'How are you, girls?'

'Ben! Lovely to see you!'

Annabel jumped up and gave him a welcoming hug. In
his tattered ex-Army Surplus overalls, his black curly hair
on end, Ben Lawrence looked more like a plumber or a
motor mechanic than a top fashion photographer. His lilting
Welsh accent and utter lack of pretension made him one of
the most popular photographers in London – and, perhaps
because he knew how to make the shyest or snootiest model
relax and smile, his pictures had a touch of magic.

'How's life? I haven't spoken to Jacqui since last week!'

'She's fine. Young Joe was a bit off-colour last week but
he's fine now, and the baby's learning new tricks every day!'

'How old are they now?' asked Suzy.

'Blowed if I can remember,' grinned Ben. 'Let me see,
Joe is four and Alice must be ...'

'She's two next month. Fine father you are!' teased Annabel.

'But I'm the proudest dad in the world,' Ben insisted, opening up the portfolio of photos he had brought with him. 'Here, look at these, girls!'

There was a set of pictures of Jacqui, laughing and radiant and looking no more than twenty, with Joe tumbling over her lap and Alice, who combined her father's jet-black curls with her mother's blue eyes, crawling towards her.

'They're beautiful,' said Annabel sincerely. 'You should be proud, Ben. You've got a smashing family!'

'Don't I know it!'

There was a knock on the door and Suzy called 'Come in!' A tall and incredibly slender black girl carrying a model book stood in the doorway.

'Annabel Lee?' she said uncertainly.

'Oh, you must be our American lady!'

'Yeah, I'm Sugarplum!'

'*Sugarplum?*'

The girl giggled. 'I'm Elly May Jones really, but they fixed me up with a fancy name when I started modelling. Here, you want to see my book? I got some great pictures, though I say it myself!'

'I must go, Annie!' said Ben, who had been looking at Sugarplum with a professional's eye, and seemed to like what he saw.

'All right, I'll come and see you out. Excuse me, Sugarplum!'

'Sure!'

'She's lovely, Annie. You'd better snap her up before someone else does,' hissed Ben in a stage whisper, when they were outside the office.

'Don't worry, I will!'

'By the way, I've got a new assistant, did I tell you?'

'Oh, that is good news. Philip only left last week, didn't he? What's this new guy like?'

'The best I've had, to be honest, Annie. Not a thought in his head for anything except taking pictures. He's from the

13

East End, a really ambitious kid. He'll go a long way, I'm sure!'

'Can't be bad!' said Annabel. 'Well, listen, Ben, we'll see you soon, OK?'

'Damn it all, now I'm about to walk out of the door without mentioning what I came to tell you,' said Ben. 'We're having a barbecue at our place on the eighteenth and of course you must come. Leonard too, if he's around. Put it down in your diary, Annie, won't you?'

'That sounds lovely. I will. 'Bye now, Ben, take care!'

2

The sun was just breaking through the clouds as Annabel edged her car out of Lauriston Mews into the tail end of the rush-hour traffic. She scrabbled in her bag for her sunglasses and balanced them precariously on her nose as she came up to the first set of traffic-lights. As she pulled away she turned the car radio on, but the inane chatter of the DJ got on her nerves, and she quickly switched over to a Dory Previn cassette. As she drove up Gloucester Place towards St John's Wood the traffic thinned out slightly and Annabel began to relax and hum along with the tape.

Leonard lived in a mansion block just off Abbey Road. Annabel parked, defiantly, in one of the spaces marked 'Residents Only'.

'Leonard! It's me!' she called, opening the front door of his flat.

Silence.

'Anyone home?'

'I'm expecting Mr Leonard at any moment, Miss Annabel!'

Mrs Elliott, Leonard's housekeeper, appeared as usual out of nowhere carrying a tea-tray and managed without saying another word to convey her disapproval of long-legged redheads in T-shirt dresses and high-heeled sandals, who had their own keys to gentlemen's apartments.

'Darling!' Leonard came in and kissed the top of her head.

'I thought I'd come straight from work and give you a surprise. I've had a hectic day!'

'Have you? Poor Annie!' He put his arms round her and

studied her intently. 'You look tired, baby. Has it been that bad?'

Annabel grinned. 'No – I am tired, but that's my own fault. Cindi came back from Dallas at three o'clock this morning and we didn't get much sleep. She's going out with some Texan with a ranch and a million head of cattle and two swimming pools and heaven knows what!'

'You women! You never miss the opportunity for a natter, do you? Even if it's three o'clock in the morning!'

'Chauvinist!' Annabel put her head on Leonard's shoulder and turned to kiss him lightly on the cheek. She could smell the expensive cologne she had given him for his birthday. For a brief moment he held her tight, then released her with a laugh.

'Is that tea just made?'

'Yes. Do you want a cup?'

Leonard watched her as she poured his tea and wondered if she would ever know how much she meant to him. Leonard Francis was a lonely man, with no family ties and few interests outside his job as manager of an import-export agency. He sometimes asked himself if he had ever really been alive before Annabel Lee had come dancing into his life, bringing youth and light and colour, laughter and, yes, love. The time he had spent as manager of his firm's Toronto branch seemed cold and colourless compared with the three years he and Annabel had been together. Looking at her, so unselfconscious and lovely in her absurdly fashionable dress, her auburn hair spilling over her shoulders, he blessed the day he'd returned to England. On an impulse, he had decided to look up his old friend Arthur Lee in Nottingham, only to be told by Arthur's widow Margaret that Arthur had died years before. Mrs Lee had added that little Anne, the daughter, Leonard remembered as a pigtailed tomboy, was now modelling in London, and had been there for four years.

'I'd be grateful if you could keep an eye on her, Leonard!'

Margaret Lee had said. 'She's a sensible girl but she's so young, and you never know these days, do you? Some of the people she works with ...'

'Of course I will!' Leonard had said. He patted her hand, dismayed at the changes he detected in his old friend's wife. Margaret Lee had always been a quiet woman, but since Arthur's death she seemed to have faded to a shadow. Only the wide green eyes and delicate bone structure remained to remind Leonard of the woman he had been half in love with, years ago.

When he met Annabel, any sentimental memories he had had of her mother disappeared like shadows in the sun. Annabel combined her mother's delicate features with her father's wavy auburn hair and a certain grace and charm she hadn't inherited from either of them. When Leonard thought back to the first evening they'd spent together he still caught his breath at the memory. He'd taken her out to his favourite restaurant. She'd worn a green dress in some filmy material that clung to her slim young body and matched her eyes. She'd made him laugh a lot, treating him like a favourite uncle ... and he had fallen utterly and irrevocably in love. For the first and last time in his life Leonard Francis knew he had met the woman who would make him whole and complete and the fact that she was young enough to be his daughter was completely irrelevant. He wanted to pick her up and protect her and care for her and beat up anyone who tried to hurt her. It was only as he came to know her better that he realized that, for all her capable and businesslike exterior, Annabel had once been badly hurt. She needed him. He knew he must tread warily, not frighten her away, not threaten her independence; and that if he could do that, one day she might be his. She had told him about Malcolm, the man who had given her her start in modelling – and broken her heart in the process.

'I'm no angel, Leonard, so don't idolize me!' she had said, her green eyes bright with the tears she was too proud to shed. 'There are always men ready to take advantage when you're modelling. I was very young, very naïve, I believed every word Malcolm said to me. Every lying word! When he left me, I promised myself I'd never love anyone again.'

'But you will, Annie. Time passes ...'

She shook her head. 'I'm not ready. When I fall in love, it's total. Total involvement, total commitment, head over heels, the whole thing. One day, maybe, I'll be ready to give someone that kind of love again, but right now I've got my work to think about!'

He had pressed his lips to the back of her hand. 'I want what you want, Annabel. I won't ever push you, I promise, but I want you to know I'm here when you need me.'

'I know. Dear Leonard, you're the best friend I've ever had!' He had not spoken of love again and gradually their relationship had developed into a loving friendship. There was affection, trust and fatherly care on his side, playfulness on hers – and if it was incomplete or unsatisfying for him, he very rarely thought of it like that. It was enough that Annabel cared for him, that heads turned when they walked into restaurants together, that his business colleagues' eyes widened with admiration when he introduced her.

'Annie, you're home now. You don't have to think about it any more. Tomorrow is another day, remember?' he said.

She smiled at him. 'I know, love. It's hard to switch off, though. That agency means so much to me ...'

'To me, too!' He ruffled her hair. 'I'm proud of my investment, Annabel, and I mean that quite seriously. I know when I suggested lending you the money to get started you weren't keen, you wanted to be independent; but quite apart from the way I feel about you, I'll never regret putting that capital into "Annabel Lee". It seems to me that you're doing a fine job!'

It wasn't just money that Leonard had put into Annabel Lee, Annabel reflected. Somehow, problems never seemed so bad when she'd told Leonard all about them. She felt safe with him, comforted by his gentle, undemanding affection.

'You're a smasher, do you know that?' she said.

'Am I?'

His brown eyes were kind. She got up and went over to curl up on the floor at his feet. He stroked her hair.

'Annabel?'

'Mmmm?'

'Why do you stay with me?'

'I'm after your money, aren't I?'

'But seriously?'

She looked up at him, smiling, noting the wrinkles round his eyes and his anxious mouth, and realizing that he was middle-aged and vulnerable and afraid of losing her.

'I think,' she said carefully, 'that we have a good thing going!'

What does he want, she thought. Does he want me to say I love him? I won't say that. I do love him, in a way ... it would make him so happy to hear me say the words. And yet, I have to be honest. I'm not ready to give him the kind of love he wants.

'Ben came into the office today,' Annabel said, when they were settled at Leonard's beautiful mahogany dining-table and Mrs Elliott had served the omelettes, together with a bottle of a delicate German wine.

'How are they all?'

'Fine. He brought in some pictures that he'd taken of Jacqui and the kids and they look wonderful. Alice is going to be as pretty as Jacqui one day, I'm sure of it. And you wouldn't believe that Jacqui was anyone's mother, let alone a little tearaway like Joe's!'

Ben and Jacqui Lawrence were among the very few of Annabel's friends who understood and appreciated the way she felt about Leonard. Annabel was sure that in the tightly-knit and gossipy world of the rag trade there were plenty of people who wondered why the glamorous Annabel Lee was involved with a man they could only see as a boring business-man, but Ben and Jacqui understood. Leonard was Annabel's protector, her escort, her father-figure, financier and friend, and she didn't feel any need to justify their relationship to anyone. She saw her girlfriends, and the models, designers and fashion journalists she worked with, fall in and out of love affairs with a selection of superficial, callous and uncaring men, and she knew that Leonard was worth ten of any of them. She smiled at him across the table.

'Philip – you know, Ben's assistant – walked out on him last week and he was going spare. You know how Ben panics!'

'What's he going to do?'

'Oh, he's got someone else already, some guy from the East End.'

'Any good?'

'Well, it's hard to tell this early, but Ben seemed pretty impressed with him so far. Maybe he'll turn out to be an-other David Bailey!'

'Another Ben Lawrence would be quite enough. Even I can see that he takes good pictures, and I'm an Instamatic man myself, as you know!'

Annabel helped herself to chocolate mousse, thanking heaven that she didn't put on weight easily. It must be hell, she thought, to be one of those models who live on a per-petual diet of cottage cheese and lettuce leaves.

'I'm glad I'm through with all that!' she said aloud.

'With all what?'

'Modelling. I don't think I'm strong-willed enough to be really good.'

Leonard raised his eyebrows. 'From what you tell me, the problem was more the other way round! You were *too* strong-willed, always telling the photographers and editors what you wanted to do instead of waiting for them to tell you! A proper little madam, Ben said!'

Annabel giggled. 'Ben was lovely to work with. He was about the only one who didn't treat me like a clothes-horse. I know I was a brat once I'd realized it was so much less glamorous than I thougth it was going to be, but that wasn't what I meant. There's no room for self-indulgence if you want to be any good in modelling. No late nights, no chocolates, no goodies at all. I haven't got that kind of self-control!'

'Oh, come on, Annie, you're still as slim as you ever were!'

'I was late in this morning, though, after burning the midnight oil with Cindi. I didn't have any appointments, luckily, but if I'd been modelling I'd never have got away with it!'

'Well, you're the boss. You can be late now and then if you like!'

She shook her head. 'Don't encourage me, Leonard. If I'm the boss I should be setting the standards for everyone else. Suzy's never late, bless her, and I scream at the models if they are. One of the first rules of professionalism is to get wherever you're going on time!'

'Professionalism is terribly important to you, isn't it?'

'Of course it is. You've got to set your own standards ...'

Leonard held up his hands in mock horror. 'All right, all right! You don't have to lecture me about professionalism and standards, especially not over dinner!'

She was instantly contrite. 'Oh, I'm sorry. I must sound like a horrid old career-woman, all strings of pearls and Chanel suits and horn-rimmed glasses. I bet that's how I'll end up!'

Leonard reached across the table and held her hand. 'You'll never be a hard career-woman to me, darling. I know there's a soft centre beneath all that professional Women's Libbery!'

Annabel looked away. 'I hate that expression, Women's Lib,' she said lightly. 'You don't need to be a fanatical feminist to run a business and you don't need to lose your femininity, either!'

21

Over coffee, Annabel suddenly remembered the barbecue. 'Will you be around on the eighteenth, love? Jacqui and Ben are having a barbecue and Ben's asked us both to come along.'

Leonard took his diary from his jacket pocket. 'Damn! I'll be away all that week, in Geneva!'

'Oh, that's a shame. I don't mind going on my own, since it's to Jacqui and Ben's, but it would have been nice if you could have been there.'

'Never mind. I'm sure you'll find some way of amusing yourself. I always feel a bit out of place at your rag-trade parties, darling. Everyone always tries desperately hard not to talk shop to me all the time, but they end up doing just that! I keep being accosted by delectable young ladies who drift away as soon as they discover that I can't get them into the movies!'

Annabel looked at him affectionately and reflected that he could very well be a film producer, except that he was slimmer and better-looking than the admittedly few of the breed she had met. His brown hair was thick and shining and just lightly frosted with grey at the temples; his lean cheeks were slightly tanned and his wide, humorous mouth made him appear rather younger than he was. When they had first met Annabel had been amused to discover that Leonard's one vanity was a point-blank refusal to reveal his exact age. It seemed an endearingly foolish weakness for such a sensible, level-headed man, so she had respected his reluctance. She could have asked her mother, sneaked a look at his passport, or tried some other subterfuge, but instead she had decided to leave it. He could be forty-five, he could be fifty-five, what did it matter?

'You should tell them you are a film producer,' she teased.

'Why would I want to do a thing like that?'

'Well, you know ... string some little dolly along a bit!'

'How many times do I have to say it, Annabel? Since you came into my life, there's been no other woman!'

22

And what can I say to that, Annabel thought. It's true, I know it is, and there must be a million women who wouldn't ask for anything more and who would be more than happy to love a man like Leonard. So why am I hesitating? Why can't I tell him that I feel the same way?

Because you don't, an honest small voice inside her said. You don't love Leonard the way you once loved Malcolm, and you care about him far to much to lie to him.

I've scared her, Leonard thought. Whenever I tell her how much she means to me I can feel her withdraw and pull away and she gets that lost remote look that turns my heart right over. Oh, Annabel, why don't you let me care for you?

'There's a nature documentary on BBC 2. Would you like to watch it?' he said.

He was rewarded with a brilliant smile and he realized, sadly, how relieved she was at his tactful changing of the subject. He sighed inwardly as he leaned over to switch on the TV. Loving Annabel on her own terms was occasionally hard, but as he looked at her, curled up on the sofa, her long legs tucked underneath her as she absent-mindedly twisted a lock of auburn hair round her finger, he knew he would never want it any other way.

If we were married, he allowed himself to fantasize, and I came home every evening to find her here like this ... but she wouldn't want that. She doesn't like this flat, I know. He glanced round the room, at the heavy antique furniture and gold brocade curtains, the fringed lampshades and the glass-fronted cabinet that housed his collection of Sèvres porcelain. He had a mental picture of Annabel's flat, all checked gingham, pine panelling and sag-bags, or of her friend Jacqui's Hampstead home with its dark brown carpets and Beardsley prints ... So, we'll move, he thought. A mews cottage, or maybe one of those modern town-houses facing Primrose Hill, whatever she wants. He knew Annabel too well to even suggest she might give up work after marriage, but one day ... She could retain a controlling interest in the agency, get someone good to run it for her when she had children. Children. A sturdy little son he could take to football matches; an auburn-curled daughter in frilled pinafores. Fantasies, sheer dreams, Kate Greenaway children, and he was a sentimental fool to believe that life could ever be like that.

'Leonard? Love, you're miles away. What is it?'

'Mmmm? What was that?'

She sounded amused. 'I said, did you realize that baby kangaroos are only about two inches long when they're born and they have to find their way up through their mother's fur to her pouch to finish growing?'

Baby kangaroos, he thought, oh, Annie ... Then suddenly he grinned and leaned over to give her a kiss.

'No, my love, I didn't know that. Today's fascinating fact!'

She pouted. 'You're teasing me! I don't believe you've been concentrating at all! I'll go home if that's how you feel!'

'I've got things on my mind too, you know,' he said gently.

'I'm a selfish bitch, aren't I?' she said, in a small voice.

He put his arms round her. 'No, you're not. You're my Annabel Lee, and I like you just the way you are!'

3

At the beginning of the next week Annabel saw Leonard off on his trip to Geneva. She had offered to come to the airport with him but he told her not to bother. He was catching an evening flight so he called in at her flat just after she had got home from work to find her and Cindi watching TV together.

'Have a good time!' she told him.

'It's work, remember, not a holiday!' he said, with a smile.

'Where is it you're going?' asked Cindi, a slim brunette with the sleek, well-cared-for look and almost permanent suntan of an air stewardess.

'Geneva.'

'Switzerland. Wow!' sighed Cindi. 'You know, I guess I ought to move around a little more and do some European routes instead of flying backwards and forwards to the good old U.S.A.'

'I'll see you when you get back, then. 'Bye, love!' said Annabel, kissing him lightly on the cheek.

'What would you like me to bring you?'

'Bring me?' said Annabel blankly.

'Yes. I'd like to get you a little present while I'm there.'

'Oh, Leonard, don't be silly. You don't have to bring me anything! You do enough for me as it is!'

Then, when she saw his crestfallen face, she relented. 'Well, maybe some perfume, I'm nearly out of my favourite.'

'Look after yourself, Annabel!'

'Don't worry, I will!'

He held her close for a moment and then was gone.

'That guy's crazy for you, Annie,' remarked Cindi casually, balancing a bottle of scarlet nail varnish precariously on the sag-bag beside her.

'So everyone keeps telling me,' said Annabel, feeling unreasonably irritated. Why did everyone have to keep on reminding her how wonderful Leonard was and how much he loved her? It only made her feel obscurely guilty for not being able to love him in quite the same way. After all, he seemed happy enough with her company, and she *was* fond of him. It was a relationship that seemed to suit them both, so why did everyone have to go on about it?

'Where are you off to next?' she asked Cindi abruptly, to change the subject.

Cindi stretched luxuriously, almost upsetting her nail varnish. 'Home to San Francisco tomorrow. I have a few days there before I fly back so I'll be able to go see Pops and Mary Lee.'

Annabel still found it a bit strange that Cindi's stepmother was younger than she was, and more like a friend to Cindi than her father's third — or was it fourth? — wife. She supposed it was the American way, but it took a bit of getting used to.

'I envy you. I could do with a holiday!'

'You must come on over some time, Annie. You'd love San Francisco, British people always do! What are you doing this weekend, while Leonard's away?'

'Jacqui and Ben are having a barbecue on Saturday. It's ages since all the crowd got together, so I'm really looking forward to it!'

'It's too bad I have to be away, really. Ben and Jacqui are real nice people.'

In fact, Annabel thoroughly enjoyed having her flat to herself. Cindi was the easiest of flatmates and Leonard the most considerate of companions, never objecting if she said she wanted a night on her own to catch up on jobs round the flat, wash her hair, or simply sit, play a few records, and dream. All the same, it was pleasant to spend Friday evening completely undisturbed, to get up late on Saturday and potter around in her housecoat, eating croissants and playing her favourite albums as loudly as she liked. She made herself a salad at lunchtime with cottage cheese and fresh pineapple, went for a jog round Regent's Park in the afternoon, washed and set her hair and then began on the difficult job of deciding what to wear for the barbecue.

Finally, she decided on her favourite green silk tunic and narrow velvet pants. She had a long, leisurely bath with bubbles up to her chin, and arrived at Jacqui and Ben's Hampstead house feeling well pleased with herself and the world. She felt a small pang of disloyalty at being so contented while Leonard was far away in Geneva, but comforted herself with the fact that he'd told her to have a good time, and would certainly not expect her to mope just because he wasn't there.

Ben opened the door. 'Annie! You look good enough to eat! Let me take your coat!'

'Nice to see you, Ben!'

Jacqui came out of the kitchen, a flowery hostess apron over her long blue caftan. 'Hello, Annie! I'm sorry Leonard couldn't come. It seems ages since we saw him!'

'Yes, he's off in Geneva, and Cindi's on a trip to San Francisco this weekend, so I'm all alone. It's quite nice actually. I can please myself what I do. Have lots of people arrived?'

'Well, it seems like hundreds, but I suppose it can't really be that many!' Jacqui smiled. 'Everyone's in the living-room, or out on the patio getting the barbecue going. I've got some sausages and some spare-ribs here I'm just going to take out. Why don't you go through and let Ben find you a drink. Louis is here, and Cathryn from *Carousel*, and Liz Watson, and Bill and Tricia.'

'Don't worry about me, Jacqui. I'll just have a wander round.'

'Here you are, a vodka and lime without you even having to ask,' said Ben, reappearing with a drink for Annabel in his hand.

'Thanks!'

Annabel went through into the living-room, saying hello to a couple of people she half-recognized on the way. It was a long, beautiful room, with cream walls, chocolate-brown carpets and a picture window at one end which opened on to the patio. Ben had strung lights round the patio and placed some of his studio floodlights further down the garden, and the effect, on this warm Spring evening, was delightful.

'Isn't that pretty!' said Annabel sincerely.

'Richard and I were out all day putting the lights up. I thought I was going to be too tired to enjoy the party!' joked Ben.

'Richard?'

'My assistant. Haven't you met him yet?'

'Oh, the new David Bailey! No, I haven't. Is he here?'

'He must be around somewhere!' said Ben, looking round. A very dark girl with dramatic eye make-up and electric blue satin jeans came up to them.

'Annie! How are you?'

'Cathryn! Good to see you! I'm glad you liked Penny Corcoran. I thought you would.'

'She's a lovely lady,' said Cathryn, who was the fashion editor of *Carousel* magazine, and had recently used one of Annabel's newest models.

Suddenly, two velvet-jacketed arms slid round Annabel's waist from behind, and someone blew softly into her ear. She wriggled free, turning, and was promptly kissed on both cheeks by a tall, lean and outrageously good-looking young foreigner.

'Annabel, chérie! When are you going to give up being a business-woman and come to Paris to work for me again?'

'Louis, you old fraud,' said Annabel, smiling. 'Anyone would think I was the best model you'd ever photographed, instead of practically the worst!'

'Darling, how can you say that?'

'Because it's true and you know it! Besides, you did nothing but scream at me or go off into sulks when I wouldn't do what you wanted me to!'

Louis looked sheepish, and then he shrugged. 'Maybe, but we are older and wiser now, darling. Anyway, if you won't model for me again, why not marry me?'

'Come off it, Louis, you know me better than that! All that Sacha Distel flattery never worked with me, did it?'

'You are the cruellest woman I ever met, Annie!'

'Nonsense! You'd have a fit if I said I'd marry you!'

Louis shook his head and kissed the tips of his fingers to Annabel as he was swept off by two tall blondes who looked like Swedish film stars.

'He's a nutcase, isn't he?' laughed Cathryn.

'Louis never changes! He will insist on putting on this dreadful artificial Frenchman act which doesn't fool anyone who's ever worked with him in Paris. It certainly doesn't fool me!'

'Annie, let me introduce you to someone nice!' said Jacqui, coming through the French windows. 'Just give me two minutes and then I promise I'll find you someone interesting to talk to!'

'It's a deal! I'm OK here for the moment, though, Jacqui.'

'Won't be long!'

Jacqui whirled off through the crowd and Annabel leaned against the wall, toying with her empty glass and wondering idly if the party was going to be as much fun as she had hoped it would be. It was nice to see the old gang; Cathryn, and Louis, but ... But what had she expected? Sir Galahad on a white horse? She gave herself a little mental shake, tossed back her thick hair, and smiled as she saw Jacqui threading her way back across the room towards her.

4

'Ben's like a ten-year-old when he gets that barbecue going!'
Jacqui grinned. 'I can hardly get him to come into the kitchen
and boil a kettle in the normal run of things, but he's turning
the spare-ribs and sausages like a proper Robert Carrier out
there! Have you had anything to eat yet, Annie?'

'Not yet. It all smells delicious, but then food cooked out
of doors always does, doesn't it? There's nothing nicer than
a barbecue on a night like this!'

'We've been hoping and praying it wouldn't rain. When it
started to cloud over this afternoon I thought we'd had it,
but it cleared up by about seven and we knew we'd be all
right.'

Annabel wasn't listening. Her attention had suddenly been
caught by a young man standing over by the stereo on the
other side of the room. He was slightly above average height,
and casually dressed in a blue fine-knit sweater and navy
corduroy jeans. He had dark blond hair, worn quite long, a
light suntan, high cheekbones, and a mouth like a sulky
angel. Annabel stared.

'Who's that, Jacqui?'

'Who?'

'The guy in the blue jumper, over there.'

Jacqui looked. 'Oh, I keep forgetting you two haven't met.
That's Richard, Ben's new assistant!'

Annabel looked again. It wasn't, she decided, his undoubted good looks that made her look twice at him. The

room was full of handsome men like Louis, with his velvet jacket and Latin charm, or even the warm and cheerful Ben. This Richard seemed something of an outsider. He wasn't talking to anyone, he wasn't dancing, he wasn't drinking. He was simply ... observing, with a detached and slightly watchful air, as if he hadn't yet decided whether to join the party or not. As Annabel watched, Cathryn James went past and said something to him. He responded politely, but without the slightest hint of flirtation. Annabel was intrigued.

'What's he like, Jacqui? As a person, I mean?'

Jacqui frowned. 'Difficult to say. He's not an easy guy to get close to. It's not that he's unfriendly, just that he always seems a bit ... remote. It's probably just dedication; he's fanatical about his work!'

'So Ben said!'

'Why, Annie, you're not taking up cradle-snatching in your old age, are you?'

'How old is he?'

'Twenty-two, I believe. Still, I can't say I blame you, love. I'd fancy him myself if he was ten years older!'

'I...'

'Annie, you're blushing!'

What on earth's the matter with me, Annabel thought, half-impatient with herself and half-amused. Anyone would think I'd never seen an attractive man before.

Suddenly, Richard was beside them.

'Annie, this is Richard Redding. Richard, Annabel Lee, my agent,' said Jacqui formally. Annabel recovered her composure, and smiled.

'Hi! Ben's told me a lot about you already.'

'Is that good or bad?' he said. He had a husky voice with a strong Cockney accent.

'Pretty good. He seems to think very highly of your work.'

'That's nice,' he said, and waited. Annabel waited too,

31

wondering if perhaps he was shy and telling herself that if he was, he would be the first shy fashion photographer that she had ever met.

'Have you...'

'Would you ...' he began, at exactly the same moment. They laughed, and suddenly the tension was broken.

'I was going to ask if you'd like a drink,' he said, indicating her empty glass.

'I'd love one.'

He put his arm lightly round her waist to steer her through the crowd, and Annabel was surprised at her strong physical response. What *is* this, she thought. It really isn't like me to be turned into a stammering schoolgirl by any man, least of all a chap a couple of years younger than me, even if he *does* look like a Greek god.

'What would you like, Annabel?'

'Vodka and lime, please!'

He brought the drink and an orange juice for himself.

'On the wagon, are you?' she said.

'No, I don't really enjoy drinking,' he replied calmly.

Annabel was even more intrigued, not so much because he was a teetotaller as because he seemed so unselfconscious about it. With most men, drinking seemed to be hopelessly bound up with their male image. Not drinking, in most men's eyes, made a man a sissy or worse. Richard Redding obviously didn't feel he had anything to prove in that direction, at least.

'Are you really Jacqui's agent? You don't look like one!'

'What does an agent look like?'

'Well, not like you!'

'Haven't you heard of the Annabel Lee Agency?'

'Oh, yes, of course. That's you, is it?'

She nodded. 'I used to be a model, but I gave it up a couple of years ago to concentrate on running a model agency instead.'

'It's pretty successful from what I hear.'

'Yes, we've been very lucky.'

'It's not just luck, though, is it? You've got to have your head screwed on right to run your own business, or you can get in no end of trouble!'

'Thanks!'

She was absurdly gratified. For some reason the awkward compliment pleased her far more than anything else he could have said. Annabel didn't need to be told she was pretty, but it was music in her ears to be told she was doing a good job. She smiled at Richard brilliantly.

'Have you had anything to eat? I was just thinking of going out to see how Ben was getting on with the barbecue!'

'Okay.'

They collected plates of spare-ribs and salad and went and sat on the steps leading down from the patio into the garden. Annabel picked at her salad, suddenly finding that she had lost interest in the food. Instead, she watched Richard ripping the meat from his spare-rib with white, even teeth, biting into a tomato, licking salad dressing from his fingers. She was acutely aware of him, lounging casually beside her. Half-shocked at herself and half-amused, she wondered what he would be like in bed.

What's the matter with me, she thought. I haven't met a man who affected me this way since – yes, since Malcolm. Fleetingly, she remembered Leonard trying to tell her that maybe, one day, she would meet someone who could give her more than he could, someone she would care about as much as she had cared about Malcolm. Oh, no, she had said, never again; it hurts too much to love that way. She had smiled and reassured him that whatever happened she would still care for him, because she couldn't imagine ever wanting any man so desperately again. She never had. Till now ...

'Messy way to eat, isn't it?' Richard grinned, licking barbecue sauce from his fingers like a schoolboy.

Annabel started on her almost untouched plate and smiled back at him. 'Mmmm. It's good!'

'Have you known Ben and Jacqui long?'

'Ever since I came to London. Jacqui and I were with the same agency, and I did my first ever trip with her. That's how we got to know each other well. It was some awful catalogue with really dreary clothes and they worked us half to death!'

'No wonder you got out of modelling!'

'Oh, it wasn't just that. I'm not as sweet-natured and easy-going as Jacqui is. My mother always used to say I was bossy, as a child, and I suppose I am a bit. At any rate, I'm a lot better as an agent than I was as a model!'

He laughed. 'Let me get you some of the French apple pie before it's all gone.'

'I shouldn't, really ...'

'I can't stand women who do nothing but diet! Go on, be a devil!'

Annabel felt young and carefree and light-hearted all of a sudden. 'All right, you've tempted me. Not too big a piece, mind!'

She watched him as he walked up the steps and across the patio and wondered why he made every other man there look so colourless. It wasn't his looks, it certainly wasn't his clothes, but there was an indefinable air of vitality and enthusiasm about him, which made the girls he passed smile invitingly and instinctively pat their hair into place, and the men look wary. He disappeared into the living-room.

'You *have* made a hit with our Richard!' Jacqui observed, sitting down beside Annabel for a moment.

'You're kidding! We've not done much more than exchange polite small-talk!' protested Annabel.

Jacqui laughed. 'You don't know what Richard's like. If he didn't like you, he'd have gone off on his own by now. I've seen it happen in the studio about six times in this past week. Looking the way he does, all the models are crazy about him, and the more they try to pin him down, the more he backs away! Ben says it's a shame that he doesn't know what he's got, but I'm not sure it's that. I think he just doesn't want to be distracted from his real love.'

'Which is?'

'Photography. Richard Redding's going to be a name to conjure with in the next few years if I know anything about it.'

'I suppose he feels safe with an old professional like me,' said Annabel bleakly. She was surprised how much she cared. After all, what did it matter what Ben's assistant thought of her?

'No, he likes you, I can tell,' Jacqui insisted.

Richard came back with two plates of apple pie.

Annabel looked up at him with the wide-eyed, appealing gaze that had never failed to fluster the most level-headed man. This time it did. Richard went on eating apple pie as if he hadn't noticed. Annabel was piqued. It was so long since she had put herself out to be charming, the least he could do was appreciate it! She leaned against him slightly and immediately felt angry with herself for being obvious. How long is it, she thought, since I needed to be obvious? 'Tell me about your job!' she said.

Was she imagining it, or was there a gleam of amusement in his eyes as he replied?

'It's exactly like any other assistant's job. Ben's very good to work for, though. I can use the studio any time I like. If you've got any new models, Annabel, I'll do some test shots for you!'

'Would you? I've just taken on a lovely American girl. She's black, and quite beautiful. She's got some great pictures from the States but she hasn't done anything here yet.'

'OK, it's a deal!'

Someone replaced the Bee Gees on the stereo with the Sex Pistols. 'Don't you like punk?' Richard said with a chuckle.

She wrinkled her nose. 'Not really. It's all a bit too noisy and tuneless for me. I like the way they've got a few girls

35

playing electric guitars in the New Wave bands, though!'

'Why shouldn't they? I'm all for equality, I must say, even though blokes moan about liberated women taking over. If I was a girl I'd want more out of life than my old lady's ever had, I can tell you!'

'You still live at home, do you?'

'Yeah. I wouldn't mind getting a flat, but it's all so expensive, and I spend most of my money on equipment. Anyway, my mum'd go spare if I left home. My brother's married and my sister lives in Newcastle, and I know she misses them.'

'What about your dad?'

'He's a funny one, the old man. Doesn't have much to say for himself. You wouldn't know he was there most of the time. He watches sport on TV a lot, has a couple of pints on a Friday night, goes to watch West Ham Saturdays, and that's his life!'

'Not for you, though?'

'No chance. I want to get away from all that. That's why I stayed on at school and went to the Tech. to do the photography course. All my old mates thought I was mad. They were all working on building sites, bringing home forty, maybe fifty quid a week – that was a few years ago now – and I never had two halfpennies to rub together, but I always knew what I wanted!'

'Do you still see those friends?'

'Now and again I do.' He laughed, without much humour. 'All in little terraced back-to-backs like my mum's, scheduled for demolition when the Council gets round to it, or stuck on the fourteenth floor of some high-rise with their wives and kids. A couple of them are divorced, even. They tell me I'm lucky!'

'Doesn't sound like luck to me. More like hard work and determination!'

'Right. I said that to Don, my best mate, once not so long ago. He's not too badly off, is Don, being in the motor trade, but he had to get married when he was eighteen and I

36

think things get a bit too much for him sometimes. He told me I was lucky to be out of it, and I said he never told me I was lucky when I was sweating away at college and he was out every night chasing the girls!'

'What did he say to that?'

'I thought he was going to thump me one at first, but in the end he said he could see what I meant!'

'It was just the same for me,' said Annabel. 'I couldn't wait to get away from Nottingham and when I got down to London I thought I was going to be the greatest model since Twiggy. It was very disillusioning when I found I hated modelling too!'

'You must have been good at it, though, to be able to afford to set up on your own,' said Richard sympathetically.

There was a sudden silence and Annabel realized guiltily that she had hardly given a thought to Leonard since she had met Richard. She had never actually told him that she wouldn't go out with anyone else. In fact, he had always encouraged her to find an escort among her male friends to take her to concerts and the theatre, or any event which didn't interest him, or which took place while he was out of the country.

'I have a backer,' she said shortly.

Richard made no comment. They sat in companionable silence for a few moments, while the party swirled around them. Through the open French windows, Annabel could see Cathryn and Louis dancing cheek-to-cheek, while one of the tall Scandinavian blondes, obviously Louis's latest girlfriend, sulked by the barbecue. Ben dashed past and winked at her. She smiled back, feeling totally at peace with her surroundings.

'Where do you live, Annabel?' Richard asked.

'I share a flat in Primrose Hill with a crazy air stewardess,' Annabel laughed.

'Oh, yes? Is she here?'

'No, she's on a flight to San Francisco this weekend.'

'That sounds great,' said Richard enviously. 'I've always wanted to travel, but the furthest I've ever been was a hitching trip on the Continent when I was a student.'

'Annabel! Darling, I haven't seen you in ages!' came a braying voice. It was Lucy Frayn, the forty-ish fashion editor of one of the popular dailies, not Annabel's favourite lady at the best of times, and the very last person she would have wanted to break up her comfortable chat with the strangely fascinating Richard Redding.

'Oh, hello, Lucy,' she said, without enthusiasm.

Lucy looked from her to Richard and back again, putting two and two together in the most irritatingly obvious way. 'I'm sorry, am I interrupting something?'

'Not at all,' said Richard. 'Actually, I promised Jacqui a dance once she'd sorted the barbecue out ... excuse me! I'll see you, Annabel!'

He smiled a polite social smile at her and strode off across the patio. Annabel felt unreasonably snubbed. He was under no obligation to spend the rest of the evening with her, and yet ...

Lucy was gazing after Richard in admiration. 'What a beautiful face that boy has! He reminds me of the young Terence Stamp, but I suppose you're too young to remember him! Who is he, Annabel?'

'Richard Redding, Ben's new assistant,' said Annabel reluctantly, hating her, and being annoyed with herself for caring at the same time.

'Of course. I'd heard Philip had left and Ben had someone new. I must apologize again for distributing your cosy little tête-à-tête, my dear!'

'Oh, nonsense, we hardly know each other!' Annabel protested.

A cloud seemed to have spread over the night sky and a breeze blew across the patio, ruffling Annabel's thin shirt and making her shiver suddenly. 'I'm going inside, Lucy, I'm getting cold.'

In the living-room, more people were dancing. The romantic music had been replaced by a disco number and as Annabel watched she noticed Jacqui and Richard dancing at the other end of the room. She had never seen a man move like that; graceful, supple without the slightest hint of effeminacy. She was fascinated.

I'm staring again, she thought impatiently. What's the matter with me? He obviously isn't interested, or he would have asked me for my telephone number. He was just being friendly, chatting to me like that. Even if we do have quite a lot in common, it doesn't mean anything. He's an interesting new face, that's all.

'Dance with me, Annie?'

It was Ben. She smiled at him and they joined the moving throng on the floor.

'What did you think of Richard?'

'He seems a nice enough guy.' There, that was just right. Quite casual, not too impressed.

'Half the models I've used this past week are crazy about him already!'

'They are?'

'I don't think any of them stand a chance, quite honestly.'

'Why not?'

'He's a funny guy, Richard. A bit of a loner, I'd say, difficult to get to know, and not very interested in chatting up women!'

'He was chatty enough with me. Practically told me his life history, in fact!'

'Did he really? He must have taken a fancy to you, then, Annie!'

The next time Annabel looked, Richard was dancing with Cathryn James, and then with Jacqui again, and then with a thin blonde in a red dress that didn't suit her. He didn't appear to have come with a girlfriend, or to be attached to anyone in particular, and Annabel noticed that it was mostly the girls who asked him to dance, rather than the other way round. One of the blonde Scandinavian girls passed out on the patio and had to be helped upstairs to Jacqui and Ben's spare room. Four-year-old Joe appeared on the stairs in his pyjamas at one point, and had to be shooed back to bed by his father and Marie–Claude, the Lawrences' plump and painfully shy French au pair. Louis and Cathryn left the party together, which probably accounted for the state of the Scandinavian girl.

'Great party, Jacqui!' Annabel said as her friend passed, her blonde hair escaping from its neat chignon and falling in loose tendrils around her beautiful face.

Jacqui squeezed her hand. 'I'm glad you're enjoying it, love. I think most people are, except for poor Tina or Lena or whatever her name is.'

'Louis is a creep,' said Annabel. 'I hope Cathryn knows what she's doing with him!'

Jacqui giggled. 'Cathryn's parents are staying with her this weekend from Wales – I bet she hasn't told Louis that! He'll drive her all the way to Chiswick and won't even get asked in for coffee. You know how tiny Cathryn's flat is, even without guests!'

'Serves Louis right,' said Annabel, with a chuckle. 'He's too smooth by half, that guy. I like him, but I wouldn't trust him as far as I could throw him!'

Suddenly, Richard appeared beside them, wearing a black leather bomber-jacket over his jeans and, Annabel instantly noted, having discarded the girl in the red dress.

'I'm off, Jacqui. Thanks for a great evening, and thank Ben for me, won't you? I can't see him anywhere.'

'He's upstairs with Joe, I think. Thanks for all your help, Richard!'

He turned to smile at Annabel. 'I'll see you around, won't I?'

'Sure to. It's a small world.'

'Nice meeting you, anyway. 'Bye now!'

Annabel watched him go. He walked with the same light

step as he danced. She noted the way his dark blond hair fell over the collar of his jacket at the back, the cut of his jeans, the way his shoes were slightly scruffy and down-at-heel...

Jacqui watched her curiously. 'There's really something about him, isn't there?' she said.

'Who? Oh ... I suppose so!'

They both laughed, and then Annabel yawned. 'Any chance of scrounging a cup of coffee off you, love? Then I really must go.'

'Of course.' Jacqui looked at her watch. 'Heavens, it's a quarter to three! Come into the kitchen and I'll put the percolator on. I'm sure lots of people would like coffee.'

When Annabel left, Jacqui and Ben came with her to the front door, and she hugged them both. 'Thanks for a lovely party. I've really enjoyed myself!'

'Sure you're OK to drive?' Ben asked.

'No problem!'

'See you, Annie!'

The door closed and Annabel walked briskly towards her car, the click of her high-heeled sandals the only sound in the silent streets. The car's engine sprang to life immediately and she drove carefully through the maze of narrow little streets that was Hampstead Village, finally turning out into Haverstock Hill and down towards Camden Town.

Yes, it had been a good party. A smattering of scandal – she grinned to herself as she pictured Louis's discomfiture when he found Cathryn's sensible, no-nonsense Welsh family bedded down in her flat – a sprinkling of gossip, a chat to Jacqui, and as an added bonus the definitely intriguing Richard Redding. Oddly enough, she found that she could remember his face perfectly; the beautiful sensual mouth and clear eyes that looked at her and yet beyond her, as if Richard refused to be bound by the limits of any situation, any country, any woman.

I'm fantasizing, she told herself. He's just a good-looking

41

young photographer with big ideas and a lot of ambition, that's all. Besides, I've got Leonard ...

Deliberately, she made herself picture Leonard instead. He'd be asleep in some Swiss hotel now; he wasn't one of the businessmen who took advantage of his expense account to sample the night-life of Europe's cities. Dear, dependable Leonard, who would no doubt bring her back some expensive, carefully-chosen and tasteful trinket as well as the perfume she had asked him for. *I wish he wouldn't*, she thought in momentary annoyance. *He always makes me feel as if I'm being bought!* Yet that was unfair to him, she knew. Leonard was simply generous; he enjoyed giving her things. What's the point of having money if you don't have anyone to share it with, he had said gently when she remonstrated with him for giving her a delicate gold chain with a tiny golden rose hanging from it. She had immediately felt ungrateful, and gave him a remorseful kiss. If it made him happy to give her things ... and she was feminine enough to love pretty jewellery and to value it as a token of Leonard's feelings for her.

I bet Richard Redding doesn't give girls gold pendants, she thought, as she parked the MGB outside her flat. Heaven help any girl who gets in the way of those restless ambitions, the need to travel, to get away and prove that a guy from Hackney could establish wider horizons.

It took Annabel a long time to get to sleep that night.

5

'Did you have a nice weekend?' said Suzy, when Annabel got to work on Monday morning.

'Yes, thanks, it was lovely. No disrespect to Cindi, but it is nice to have the place to myself once in a while, so I can be a slob if I want to!' laughed Annabel.

'She must be away quite a lot, though, isn't she?'

'Yes, but this weekend Leonard was away too.'

'Oh, Annie, poor Leonard!'

'I didn't mean that ...'

'No, it's all right, I know you didn't. Sometimes I wonder if you really appreciate that guy, though!' said Suzy severely.

Annabel reflected, guiltily, that Suzy was probably quite right. It wasn't that she wasn't looking forward to seeing Leonard when he returned from his business trip, just that she hadn't really missed him. I am a bitch, she thought, I don't deserve him.

'How was the barbecue?'

'Great! Jacqui and Ben's parties are always good. They seem to take that little bit more trouble to get everything just so, and it was such a beautiful evening. We were very lucky!'

'Who was there?'

'Oh, just the usual crowd. Louis was over from Paris, and Cathryn James, and Lucy Frayn –'

'Your favourite lady!' Suzy chuckled. 'Did you meet Ben's assistant, Annabel?'

Annabel's heart began to thump, slowly and painfully, and

her stomach lurched as if she were going down too fast in a lift.

'Ben's assistant?' she stammered. 'Er ... yes, yes I did. Why do you ask?'

Suzy looked puzzled. 'It's only that Claire Traynor rang in this morning just before you got in. She did a session with Ben last Friday, you know. I asked her how it went and she never stopped raving about this ... what's his name ...'

'Richard. Richard Redding,' said Annabel automatically.

'Oh, yes, that's right. Well, Claire kept on and on about how good-looking he was and I wondered what you thought of him?'

'He seemed very pleasant.'

'Claire made him sound like Robert Redford and Clint Eastwood rolled into one! Did you think he was good-looking?'

'I suppose so.'

Suzy laughed. 'You're a one-man girl, aren't you, Annie?'

I'm beginning to wonder, Annabel thought, disturbed. Whatever is the matter with me? I've only met the guy once and I'm carrying on like a lovesick teenager. It's ridiculous. So, Richard Redding is a good-looking guy and I enjoyed talking to him. I know dozens of good-looking men who are pleasant company, so why does this particular one make me feel so ... uneasy?

Leonard came back from Geneva on Wednesday. He called Annabel from the airport and promised to take her out for a celebration dinner on Thursday evening.

'What are we celebrating?' asked Annabel, smiling.

'Well, I've done some good deals,' said Leonard cheerfully, 'or we can celebrate my homecoming, or sunny weather, or the fact that it's Thursday the twenty-third, or anything you like!'

His gaiety was infectious and Annabel laughed. 'OK, love. Pick me up at eight at the flat, then.'

She took special care with her appearance on Thursday evening, wearing a cream silk dress and the tiny golden rose pendant that Leonard had brought her back from an earlier trip. I'm too pale, she thought, gazing at her reflection in the bedroom mirror. Maybe I need a holiday, and that's why I've been so jumpy lately.

'You look gorgeous, Annie!' Leonard said, giving her a gentle kiss on the cheek.

'You don't look so bad yourself!' she teased him. He was wearing a lightweight suit and a shirt in her favourite shade of peacock blue. He followed her into the living-room and promptly presented her with a small and a large box, gift-wrapped by a Geneva department store.

'Oh, Leonard, you are good to me!' said Annabel weakly.

His face softened, and he smiled at her. 'I think you're worth it! Come on, open them!'

The smaller package contained a huge flask of her favourite perfume. Leonard was the sort of man who never had to ask twice what her favourite scents or flowers or chocolates were. In the large box was a caftan in the sheerest Swiss cotton lawn, delicately embroidered at the neck and sleeves in blue. Annabel held it up against herself. 'Leonard, it's beautiful!'

'You like it? I hoped you would!'

'It's ... about the prettiest thing I ever saw!' She hugged him impulsively. 'Bless you, love.'

For a long moment he looked deep into her eyes, searching for something that went deeper than affection, than gratitude ... and then she looked away.

'Come on, love, let's eat. I'm starving!'

The next day, the new issue of *Lady Fair* was on the bookstalls. Annabel bought one before she set out for work, as Jacqui was on the cover and also in a fashion spread inside. Looking at her friend's classically beautiful face, Annabel realized again that Jacqui was one of the few models who could go on working for ever. She certainly didn't look like the twenty-six-year-old mother of two children.

As soon as she had got into the office, she telephoned Ben.

'Ben? It's Annie! Listen, have you seen the new *Lady Fair*?'

'Not yet. That's the Hampstead Heath session, isn't it?'

'Yes, and Jacqui looks wonderful. I've got it right here. Actually, Ben, I was wondering if I might pop over with it at lunch time. Will you be at the studio?'

'Sure. I'm not shooting today, as it happens. I might even buy you a drink, seeing as it's you!'

Ben Lawrence's studio was in a quiet Mayfair street, not too far from Annabel's office. As it was sunny and she was wearing her most comfortable sandals, she decided to walk. London was really lovely at this time of year, she thought, without the dusty, jaded look or the crowds of tourists that high summer inevitably brought. A couple of workmen on a building site whistled at her. She strode on with her nose in the air, but she couldn't help smiling. When all was said and done, it was nice to be twenty-four and pretty and have a business of your own and be going to have lunch with a good friend like Ben ...

And see Richard Redding again? said her conscience.

Oh, nonsense, thought Annabel. That's not why I'm going to Ben's at all. I just want to congratulate him on these lovely pictures. What do I care if Richard Redding's there?

He wasn't. Annabel looked round Ben's studio, with its inevitable clutter of props and equipment, and wondered if her absurd, ludicrous disappointment showed in her face.

'Not bad, are they?' said Ben, flicking through the magazine.

'Jacqui looks just as lovely as she did the day I met her,' said Annabel sincerely, wondering where Richard was.

Settled in the comfortable bar of Ben's local with a half of lager and a ploughman's lunch, Annabel plucked up the courage to ask about him.

'I sent him out to show his book to one or two magazine

editors,' said Ben, 'since we're not busy today. He hasn't done all that much yet, of course, but they might as well get to know him. He's a nice guy, isn't he, Annie?'

'Yes ... yes, he is. He seemed very dedicated,' said Annabel.

'You're not kidding. Richard Redding intends to make it to the very top and I wouldn't like to be the one to stop him. He's got the right sort of single-mindedness, too. I mean, if I want to go away, I've got to think about Jacqui and the kids, but Richard wouldn't even let his family stand in his way!'

'He's *married*?'

'No, no – or not as far as I know! Richard never talks about his personal life much. I just meant that work comes first with him.'

'I see.'

Ben and Annabel chatted amiably, and had a couple of drinks each, and then she looked at her watch.

'Half-past two!' she gasped. 'Suzy'll be wondering where I've got to. I'd better get a cab back. Thanks for the drink, Ben.'

'Any time, sweetheart.'

She kissed him, and left. Outside in the street she stood hopefully by the side of the road waiting to hail a taxi, but the few that passed were all full.

'It's Annabel, isn't it?'

He was beside her, smiling at her, and her throat contracted. 'Oh! Er ... hi, Richard!'

'Been up to the studio, have you?' he enquired pleasantly.

'Yes, I took Ben the new *Lady Fair* with his pictures in.'

'I must have a look, see if I can learn something!'

Silence. Annabel hurriedly cast about in her mind for something amusing or fascinating to say, and drew a complete blank. She looked at him. He was wearing faded denim jeans and a black leather jacket, and he was more tanned and better-looking than she remembered ... not as tall,

47

perhaps, and his eyes were cool and grey. She'd remembered them as blue. The beautiful sulky mouth was the same, though. She imagined tracing its outline with her finger, and felt herself grow hot with embarrassment, realizing that she was staring.

'Nice to see the sun, isn't it?' he said.

'Oh, yes. I walked over, actually, but I'll get a cab back, to save time.'

'Where's your office, Annabel?'

'Lauriston Mews, over Paddington way.'

'That's quite a walk!'

'I like walking, if the weather's nice.' God, she thought, what a fatuous thing to say. I must sound like an idiot. Whatever will he think of me?

'Do you still want me to take some pictures of your new model?' he asked, and she took refuge in professional briskness.

'Oh, yes, Sugarplum. That would be great.'

'When?'

'Well ... any time you're free, really. Sugarplum's not working much at the moment. She's doing a fashion show next week, on Thursday I think, but apart from that, any day.'

'It will have to be in the evening. Ben says that after six I can use the studio any time, unless he's working, of course.'

'OK. Do you want to call me and confirm which day you can do it?'

'Fine. Ben's got your number, hasn't he?'

'Yes.'

Silence again. Annabel felt even more foolish. What *was* there about this man that disturbed her so?

'There's a taxi, Annabel!'

He hailed the cab for her and held the door open while she climbed in. Oh, that smile, Annabel thought, I can see what young Claire Traynor meant. She felt warm and young and silly as she grinned at him. 'See you, then!'

48

She took the stairs at the office two at a time, flung her bag down on her desk, and smiled sunnily at Suzy and Gillian, who was making coffee.

'Sorry I'm late, everyone. I went out to the pub with Ben!'

'However much did you have to drink, Annie? You're glowing!' teased Suzy.

Annabel blushed. 'Oh, not much. It's just such a beautiful day! Has Sugarplum got any bookings apart from that fashion show next week?'

Suzy took the girl's card from the index. '*Fancy* want to use her on Tuesday morning, but that's only half a day. Why?'

'Ben's assistant wants to do a session with her, that's all.'

Suzy looked at her sharply but Annabel's face gave nothing away.

'He's going to call at the beginning of the week, when he knows when Ben's going to be out of the studio.'

Driving back to Primrose Hill that evening, Annabel felt unexpectedly light-hearted. She parked the car and went into the flat to find a note from Cindi: 'Out for dinner with P.' P? Would that be Peter, the Deep South co-pilot, or Paul, the record producer from Coventry? Cindi's love-life was endlessly complicated. Air stewardesses seemed to be the female version of the sailor with a wife in every port.

An hour later, Annabel emerged pink and glowing from the bathroom to wrap herself in her white towelling bathrobe and settle on to a sag-bag with a couple of magazines. Even now, when she was relaxing, she couldn't help looking with professional interest at the models, the photography and the locations in the fashion features. She was mildly interested to see Ellie Fitton, who had started modelling at the same time as she had, on the cover of one of the magazines. She flicked it open at an article headed, 'Do you need more than one lover?' and closed it again, hastily.

No, she thought, I've got Leonard and everyone keeps telling me he's all I need ... but she was too honest to hide the attraction she felt towards Richard Redding from herself any longer. Tonight's good spirits could only be because she knew she would be seeing him, speaking to him, again soon. And let's hope I don't make quite such an idiot of myself next time, she thought. It's quite amusing, really. People would laugh if they knew. The cool, capable Annabel Lee with a crush on a photographer's assistant! It *was* funny. It was a joke ... wasn't it?

In the event it was Ben Lawrence who called Annabel to tell her that the studio would be free for Richard the following Wednesday evening, and if Sugarplum could be there at half-past six they could do an evening session.

'You'd better come with her, Annie,' Ben suggested, 'if you don't mind, that is. Richard's got a friend helping him and I'd feel a lot happier if your lady had you with her, just till they break the ice and start working properly. Richard knows his way around a camera, all right, but I can see new models finding him a bit forbidding to work with. He doesn't go out of his way to put them at their ease!'

'Sugarplum's not exactly new,' Annabel laughed. 'She's already worked a couple of years in New York, but I'll drop her round in the car on my way home, if you like.'

'This guy's new, is he?' drawled Sugarplum, curled up in the passenger seat of Annabel's car, her model bag on her lap.

'New, but very promising, Ben says,' Annabel assured her.

Richard seemed to have everything ready when the two girls arrived.

'Richard Redding – Sugarplum, from New York!' said Annabel formally.

'Macon, Georgia via New York!' the girl corrected her.

'Pleased to meet you,' said Richard, looking her up and

down with professional, rather than personal, interest. 'Thank you, Annabel!'

'Mind if I stay around for a while? It's ages since I sat in on a session,' asked Annabel casually.

'If you like.'

She felt snubbed. Sugarplum went to the little room off the studio to change and Annabel watched idly as Richard moved the lights around with the help of a thin young man in punk-style clothes whom he briefly introduced as Fred. Sugarplum emerged, dressed in a bright pink leotard and footless tights.

'Where do you want me, Richard?'

'We'll start with some static shots, I think. Come over here ... now just stand, like that ... shoulders back ... head on one side ... that's lovely. Now, head up ... look over your shoulder, no, not too much ... fine, now you can open your mouth slightly, yes, that's fine ...'

He was totally absorbed, and Annabel felt she was in the way, even though neither Richard, Fred or Sugarplum took the slightest notice of her. I'll go in a minute, she thought. There's nothing more I can do here and I'll only be a nuisance when Sugarplum starts moving around. She watched Richard, concentration in every line of his face and body, hunched over the camera, completely involved. I might as well not have come, she thought dismally. He'd been polite, but no more than that, so that the rapport they had established so briefly at the barbecue seemed like a figment of her imagination. When they took a break, she said, 'I think I'll leave you to it, if everything's OK?'

'Fine,' said Sugarplum, smiling.

'Yeah, no problem. Goodbye, Annabel!'

That was that, then. Total indifference. She might just as well have been the motherly, middle-aged figure he'd obviously expected an agent to be. He'd certainly shown no signs of finding her attractive, or even particularly interesting.

Still, why should he, thought Annabel, depressed. He works surrounded by beautiful women all day. Why should he notice me, especially?

She drove home slowly. Early summer evenings seemed to encourage lovers to dawdle along the pavements, hand in hand, arm in arm, whispering. Annabel experienced a sudden pang of loneliness, and abruptly turned the car into a side-road leading to St John's Wood and Leonard. At least he appreciates me, she thought. No, that's not fair. I mustn't use Leonard to boost my morale because Richard doesn't want me.

It sounded so bald, put like that. Richard didn't want her. He didn't want her, Annabel Lee, who had had men running after her ever since she had discarded her childhood pig-tails. She remembered the boys from the Grammar School at home, blushing and stammering and offering to carry her books. Keith, her first boyfriend, kissing her with his soft, beardless lips in the back row of the Odeon, and writing her pages of lovesick poetry after she told him she didn't want to see him any more. And when she came to London, there had been an endless stream of young men – photographers, journalists, designers, actors, people in the music business – all more than willing to escort a leggy red-haired model to clubs and restaurants and parties. She had chosen Malcolm, older than the rest, who seemed to her inexperienced seventeen-year-old eyes to be everything she had ever dreamed of in a man, with his Gucci shoes and tasteful French clothes.

'We'll be so good together, you and I, baby!' he had whispered to her, dazzling the starry-eyed Nottingham school-girl who still remained beneath the veneer of London sophistication. And she remembered the way it had ended: Malcolm's cold, totally uninterested voice as she had wept at him over the telephone.

'No, I'm sorry, baby, but it's better this way!'

'But how can it be better? I love you!'

'That,' he said lightly, 'is your misfortune. You take life too seriously, Annabel!'

Annabel accelerated sharply, remembering. She *had* taken life seriously then. And it had been a mistake, and a painful one, to take a man as calculating and superficial as Malcolm Roberts seriously.

But at least he fancied me, she thought. Richard Redding doesn't, and for once in my life I have no idea what to do about it. I thought I had all the answers, didn't I? I could never understand the girls who got hung up about a man. If you want him, go get him; if you don't, forget him. I really thought it was that simple! I've thought of nothing else but Richard Redding ever since I met him. I expected him to ask for my telephone number, call and ask me out, whatever. I expected him to notice me, but I don't know if he even does that!

In the close-knit world of the rag trade it was hard for Annabel to avoid seeing Richard, even if she had wanted to. Over the next few weeks he seemed to be everywhere: at fashion shows, at the party given by a magazine publishers to launch a new title, even once in the 'Annabel Lee' office to deliver his photographs of Sugarplum.

Annabel even caught herself making excuses to drop in at Ben's studio to deliver cheques and magazines that she could quite easily have sent by post. He was always there, always polite and friendly, but giving no sign that he thought of her as anything more than a business colleague and casual acquaintance.

I'm running after him, Annabel thought, tormenting herself. How everyone must laugh! Everyone must have noticed, except Richard. Why doesn't he see that I'm always around? Suppose he does notice? Suppose he knows, and thinks it's funny, or embarrassing. I couldn't bear that!

Then, one Saturday, she met him quite by chance in Covent Garden. She had gone there partly to look for some new clothes for work, and partly just to browse. Since the market had moved to Nine Elms, new shops and restaurants seemed to open and close almost every week. Annabel was outside a pottery shop when she saw an instantly recognizable reflection in the window beside her. As always when she saw Richard, her heart beat fast, her knees went weak, and she felt about fifteen.

'Hello, there!' he said pleasantly.

'Oh, hi,' she said with studied casualness. 'What brings you round here?'

'I often come on Saturdays and have a wander round,' he said. 'I really love this area. I wouldn't mind getting my own studio here one day.'

'One or two photographers I know do have studios here. It's a super part of London to work in.'

He fell into step beside her, easily and naturally. 'Are you looking for anything special?'

'Well, I thought I might try and get some clothes,' said Annabel, wishing she was wearing something more exotic than last year's jeans and an old red T-shirt one of Cindi's boyfriends, who worked for a rock band, had given her.

'You should wear that silky shirt thing you wore at the barbecue more often,' he said matter-of-factly. 'Green's your colour, Annabel!'

Annabel was too amazed to retort that redheads were always expected to look good in green. It was the first sign Richard had ever given her that he noticed how she looked, what she wore, or anything about her.

'I like green,' she said, rather feebly, 'but that shirt's real Thai silk. I wouldn't wear it for messing about on a Saturday!'

'What do you generally do on Saturdays?'

She shrugged. 'Mess about!'

They both laughed. Annabel wondered, suddenly, if he

54

had a girlfriend, tucked away in Hackney somewhere. That would explain his apparent lack of interest in the girls he worked with – and in herself.

'Are you meeting someone?' she enquired artlessly.

'Nope!'

'All alone, then?'

'Yes, I enjoy my own company!'

That was that, Annabel thought forlornly. They came to the junction of Endell Street and Long Acre, and as she turned into Long Acre Richard said, 'I'm going this way, Annabel!' and made to cross the road.

'Oh. Well, I'll see you around!'

'Nice meeting you, anyway. I hope you get what you want!' He smiled easily at her, and was gone.

Oh, well, Annabel thought, at least he said it was nice meeting me. And he remembered what I wore at the barbecue. I'm making progress. Well, a bit of progress, anyway ...

6

People who talk about *just* infatuation, Annabel thought miserably, are talking through their hats. The way she felt about Richard Redding was no more than a teenage crush, but it was ridiculously, impossibly painful, all the same. She felt so foolish when she caught herself scribbling his name on scraps of paper, jumping each time the telephone rang, drifting off into daydreams in the office. She lost her appetite, and couldn't sleep. She was touched to the point of tears by clichéd pop records she would have dismissed as sentimental rubbish two short months ago.

A week when she could find no excuse to pop down to Ben's studio meant misery. A week when she could, meant misery, too, because Richard treated her with exactly the same impersonal friendliness he used towards Ben, Jacqui, or the models he worked with. Time and time again, she would come away vowing to forget all about him, and being furious with herself for creeping back, each time, like a lovesick schoolgirl. If he touched her arm in passing, she tingled all over. If he smiled at her, she glowed, and her urgent, primitive need to touch him and be close to him seemed most embarrassing of all.

She couldn't bring herself to confide in Jacqui, or Ben, though she thought that they must surely have noticed. They're too kind to laugh at me, though, she thought, humiliated. The Ice Maiden, the boys used to call me when I was modelling; cool Annabel Lee who never let any man get under her skin. If it was *just* infatuation, why did it hurt so much?

Leonard was too perceptive, and too much in love with Annabel, not to notice that something was very wrong. She kept making excuses not to see him, and she never dropped in at the end of the day to talk things over with him, as she used to do.

'Annie, look at me!' he said once, taking her in his arms.

She looked. He saw the dark circles round her beautiful eyes, felt the tension in her slim body and clenched hands. Something is tearing her apart, he thought sadly, and she won't let me help her with it, whatever it is.

'Something's wrong, Annie. Is it anything I've done?'

'No, of course not,' she said wearily. 'You've been wonderful, you always are. It's just ... oh, it's all such a mess!'

He held her, gently, while she cried. Annabel hardly ever cried, and it disturbed him more than he had thought possible.

'Can't you tell me?'

She shook her head.

'Why not?'

She looked at him dumbly. Why not? Because he didn't deserve that. Because she was afraid he would laugh. Because she was afraid he would turn away from her, and she needed him. Because even Leonard wouldn't be able to imagine her, Annabel Lee, hopelessly infatuated with someone who barely knew she existed. He would probably find it inconceivable that Richard wasn't interested, which was the dreadful irony of it all. How could she tell him that?

'I don't want to keep pressing you,' said Leonard, 'if you really want to get through it on your own, whatever it is. But –'

'Yes?'

'I want you to know that I'm here if you need me. If you want help, sympathy, a shoulder to cry on, anything, that's what I'm for. You don't have to tell me what's upsetting you like this. If you'd rather not see me, even, till you've sorted it out, that's all right by me, too.'

'Oh, Leonard, you're ... unbelievable. I don't deserve you!'

He kissed the top of her head. 'Nonsense. I'm a volunteer, remember? Anything I do for you, I do because I want to. I'm basically highly selfish, and I like having you around! But I want my happy girl back, don't I?'

Although she was having trouble sleeping, during the daytime Annabel was filled with a restless energy. She stopped day-dreaming in the office, and worked harder than ever, even reorganizing her slightly haphazard filing system and copying the addresses in her tatty old address book into a smart new one. At lunchtime and in the evenings, she walked. Regent's Park and Primrose Hill were her favourites, and convenient. Along the Inner Circle, past the giraffes, the open-air theatre, the rose gardens, thinking, always thinking.

I'll get over this, of course I will. Heavens, I'm supposed to be a mature adult. These things happen. It could have been anyone. He can't be interested, or he'd have rung me. He just thinks of me as the boss of 'Annabel Lee'. But he did remember what I wore at the barbecue. We seemed to hit it off, there. We seemed to have a lot in common. I'm not imagining it.

She would arrive back at the flat, exhausted, make a drink and flop into bed to toss and turn for a couple of hours before falling into an uneasy, dream-filled sleep.

Ben and Jacqui went on a fashion trip to the West Coast of the U.S.A. with one of the glossy monthlies.

'Take care of yourself, Annie. You look like you're over-working to me,' said Jacqui, giving her a parting hug.

'Why don't you try and get away for a few days? Take a break, it'll do you good!'

'Maybe I will.'

As it happened, Annabel felt that the last thing she needed

was a break. Too much time to relax and do nothing, too much time to think.

'Damn! I forgot to send this cheque to Ben before he left!' said Suzy, in the office one day. 'I know he was waiting for it; what a bore!'

An idea began to take shape in Annabel's mind, but before she could put it into words, Suzy said it for her.

'I wonder if Richard would mind banking it for Ben?'

'I could pop round there on my way home and ask, if you like,' said Annabel, careful to keep her voice light and casual.

'Would you mind? I meant to take it last week!'

'No, it's no trouble.'

One more time, Annabel told herself, as she drove round to Ben's after work that night. Maybe I'll find it easier to talk to him now there's no one else there. Unless he's doing a session or something and the studio's full of giggling models ...

Richard was alone when she arrived. He smiled at her and she was struck, as she frequently was when she saw him, by the crazy artificiality of it all. Here he is, this guy I've been losing my sleep over, and we're chatting like two strangers at the vicar's tea-party!

'I brought this cheque in; I know Ben was expecting it,' she said apologetically. 'I wondered if you'd mind banking it for him?'

'Sure. Thanks, Annabel!'

She looked round. 'Are you busy? Working tonight?'

'No, just clearing up, really. Ben left the place in a bit of a mess! He did a session the other day with three hundred red balloons, so I spent all Wednesday night blowing them up and all today popping them! There are bits of balloon everywhere!'

'You really are dedicated, aren't you?' Annabel said, look-

59

ing up at him under her eyelashes. So what if I make it obvious, she thought recklessly. Being subtle hasn't got me very far! 'Ben tells me you're often here until ten or eleven at night!'

'I'm happiest here,' he said quietly.

'Doesn't your girlfriend mind you working so late?'

There was a silence. Annabel held her breath.

'I haven't got a girlfriend.'

'Well, your family, then? Your friends?'

'I'm not a very sociable person,' he said with an effort. 'Oh, I used to be when I was younger. All us lads used to go around together to dances, getting drunk, picking fights, chasing girls; but you grow out of that, don't you? It's a way to prove yourself, kind of, and I don't need that any more. Besides, like I said, my friends are mostly married.'

'You've never fancied getting married, then?'

'Me? You're joking!'

'Why?'

He grinned at her, and it was as if he were seeing her for the first time. Annabel felt a blush simmer up the back of her neck, and cursed the habit she kept hoping she'd grow out of.

'I'm not the type to settle down. I want to travel, and I want to make it as a photographer. That doesn't sound much like the recipe for a happy married life, does it?'

'Well, if you met the right person ...' said Annabel awkwardly, feeling like a matchmaking elderly aunt, and wondering for the hundredth time what it was about Richard Redding that made her instinctively say the wrong thing.

'She'd have to be a Supergirl, I reckon, to put up with me!' he said easily. 'Want a cup of coffee, Annabel?'

'Thanks, I'd love one.'

He made two mugs of Instant, and brought one over to where she was sitting on Ben's sagging old velvet-covered sofa. She was flicking through the pages of a magazine with some more of Ben's photographs in.

'Jacqui looks good, doesn't she?' he said, handing her her coffee. She felt an unreasonable pang. Maybe he fancies her, she thought. Why not? They are together a lot and she's so beautiful ...

'She always looks good, though.' He sat down beside her and she was instantly aware of his physical nearness. He wore jeans, as usual, and a faded cotton T-shirt. There was stubble on his chin, as if he hadn't bothered to shave that morning ... or perhaps he needed to shave twice a day? His hair was untidy, too. Annabel stifled a sudden impulse to run her fingers through it. Now what, she thought. It's his move.

Richard drained his coffee. 'Time to go home, I think. Can I give you a lift anywhere?'

Annabel's heart sank. 'No thanks, I've got my car outside.'

'Let me just make sure I haven't left any lights on.'

He got up and disappeared into the other room. On a sudden impulse, Annabel scrabbled in her bag for a pen and a piece of paper. Quickly, she scrawled her Primrose Hill telephone number and her name, and without really thinking about it slipped it into the pocket of Richard's black leather jacket, which was lying on the arm of the sofa. It was all done in a few seconds, and she sat back, her hands shaking.

'Everything's off. Coming?' He picked up his jacket and slung it casually over his shoulder. Once outside, she got into her MGB and he got into an extremely battered grey 2CV van.

'Nice motor, yours,' he said from the window.

She shrugged, self-deprecatingly. 'Yours has lots more character, though!'

He grinned. 'It goes, that's all I care about. See you, Annabel!'

Annabel roared away, unable to resist showing off just a little, and the last thing she heard was Richard's van putt-puttering out into the main road.

What have I done? she thought. Suppose he doesn't ring?

I'll never know if he found it or not. Suppose he does ring? What shall I say? Oh, help, how do people cope with this sort of thing? I thought I was sophisticated enough to handle anything. I'm twenty-four, for heaven's sake, too old to fall to pieces over a guy like that. Well, if nothing else, this whole silly episode has shown me I'm not nearly as good at coping with men as I thought I was. Maybe it's been worth it, to find that out ... will he ring me? What shall I say when he does? I've burned my boats now, no use in wishing I hadn't. Nothing venture, nothing gain, and whatever happens it can't be any worse than the last couple of months have been.

Driving home, she felt oddly calm, and that night she slept without dreaming.

The next day, she rushed home from work at six o'clock.

'You're early!' said Cindi, surprised in heated rollers, a face pack, and Annabel's towelling bathrobe.

'Yes, well, I'm expecting an important phone call,' said Annabel, too jittery to bother making up some story. Besides, Cindi's own love-life was unconventional enough for her to take Annabel's in her stride.

'You don't say. Who is he?'

Annabel grinned. 'Who said it was a he? Could just be business!'

'Then why doesn't he call you at the office? No, I smell intrigue!'

'You should know!' Annabel teased.

'You're not saying, huh?'

'Cindi, there's nothing to say, cross my heart!'

At that moment, the telephone rang. Annabel broke all records dashing across the hall to pick it up.

'Double seven o three ... yes?' Wordlessly, she held out the phone to Cindi. 'It's for you!'

'Can't,' mouthed Cindi, 'my facepack's hardening! Tell whoever it is I'll call back!'

By eight o'clock Cindi had gone out and Annabel was

keeping her vigil alone. The phone rang at eight-thirty; it was her mother. Distracted (supposing he tries to get through, and the line's engaged?), Annabel held a half-hearted conversation with her. Ten minutes later it rang again, this time for Cindi. Annabel switched on the TV and tried to get absorbed in the play. Come on, come on, telephone, she thought. It rang again at nine forty-five; wrong number. Annabel had a bath, to encourage it to ring again. It didn't. At eleven-thirty, her eyes stinging with hopeless tears, she got ready for bed. Unbelieving, she heard the telephone again, just as she was getting into bed. This time she let it ring while she found her slippers.

'Annie? It's Richard!'

She wanted to scream, turn a somersault, jump up and down, but instead she simply said, 'Richard. Hello!' She caught sight of her Cheshire-cat grin in the mirror above the telephone table, and stuck her tongue out at herself.

'I got your note ... did I wake you?'

'No, I wasn't asleep.'

'I was hanging my jacket up and it fell out of the pocket. I rang you straight away.'

'It was a bit naughty of me. Ladies aren't really supposed to take the initiative like that,' she said demurely, and heard him chuckle at the other end of the line.

'I'm very glad you did. Can we meet?'

She felt light-headed with relief. She had been forward, obvious, 'fast', all the things her mother had warned her not to be, and it didn't seem to matter.

'Name the day!'

'Tomorrow.'

'Why not?' Any appointments would just have to wait.

'Where?'

Annabel thought of all the obvious places: her flat, the office, Ben's studio, and rejected them all. She didn't want to be the focus of a lot of rag-trade gossip, to have her life dissected and commented upon by strangers, acquaintances, even friends. She was about to join the ranks of the unfaithful, the discreet thousands who snatch anonymous meetings in faceless pubs and nameless parks, and she was too dizzy with happiness to care. 'Trafalgar Square,' she said. 'By the lions. Half-past twelve.'

'I'll be there,' said Richard, and rang off.

She told Suzy she had a lunch appointment, and took the Underground to Charing Cross. She was wearing a simple green cotton dress. ('Green's your colour, Annabel!') She felt like a teenager on her first date. Her palms were damp, and butterflies careered around in her stomach. When she arrived at Charing Cross her legs felt like lead. Somehow, they carried her forward across the Strand and into the square.

He wasn't there. It's all a joke, or a dream, she thought. He's not coming, he's thought better of it, he's late ... or am I early? I'll walk once round the fountains, and if he's not there by then I'll ... well, I'll walk round the fountains again, that's all.

And then she saw him. He was walking, no, he was running down the steps and towards the lions. Oh, he's beautiful, Annabel thought wildly. Her heart seemed to turn right over and began to thump, slowly and painfully. Her stomach contracted, her knees went weak and she felt an enormous, idiotic smile spread right across her face. I don't believe this, she thought, stunned by the strength of her feelings. People don't really feel like this about people, not in real life.

'Annie.' He was there, he was smiling at her.

'Richard,' she said, and fell into his arms. The crowds of tourists and passers-by and pigeons simply faded away, and they could have been the only two people on earth. Afterwards, when Annabel tried to recall that first meeting, she found she could remember very little about it. Somehow, holding hands and laughing like a couple of schoolchildren playing truant, they dodged across the road through the

64

traffic and went into St James's Park. They bought ice-creams, and sat on the grass to eat them. There seemed no need for explanations; all she wanted to do was to be close to him, to convince herself that he was really there.

'What did you think when you found my note?' she asked him, secure in this new intimacy.

'That I was lucky. What else?'

'But you never seemed to be ... I mean, why didn't you call me before?'

'I heard you were practically engaged. To some rich businessman, they said.'

'Who told you that?'

He shrugged. 'Can't remember. It might have been Claire.'

Annabel was silent for a moment.

'Is it true?' he asked.

'I don't see how anyone can be practically engaged,' she objected. 'I do have a very ... close relationship with Leonard, but he's never mentioned getting married or anything like that. It's not that sort of a relationship, really. He's more like – not exactly my father, but an uncle or godfather or something.'

'Do you love him, Annie?'

'Well, yes. I suppose I do. In a way. I need him, and we get on very well, we always have. Do you believe me?'

'Why shouldn't I?'

'Some people might say I couldn't want anyone else if I really loved Leonard.'

He made a small impatient movement. 'I don't reckon anything is ever that simple, is it? It seems to me that we make things ten times harder for ourselves by putting everything into a category, and setting limits to our feelings.'

She felt an enormous sense of relief and kindred-spiritship with him. 'But that's exactly how I feel! I'm terribly fond of Leonard, but that doesn't stop me from wanting to see you, too!'

He smiled. 'That's called having your cake and eating it,

too. Most people would do it that way, if they could.'

'But how about you? Isn't there anyone else in your life?'

'No, no one else.'

They were both silent for a moment and then he said, 'I'm kind of a weirdo, Annie, or that's what people tell me. I like my own company, I like to please myself what I do. It's very important to me to feel free.'

'To me, too!' she assured him.

'Do you really mean that?'

'Why shouldn't I?'

'It seems to me that most women don't really know what they do want. You start off agreeing not to tie each other down, and the next thing you know she wants to know exactly what you're doing every minute of the time you're not together, and starts going on about rings and three-piece suites.'

'Oh, come on. Aren't you being a bit old-fashioned? Most of the girls I know are dead keen to get on. I know I am!'

'Not where I come from they're not. Round Hackney, girls start getting worried if they're not married by eighteen, or engaged at least!'

Annabel remembered the oohs and aahs and envious glances her fellow fifth-formers had given to the first girl in the class to come in sporting an engagement ring on a ribbon round her neck. 'Well, maybe some of them *do* still think that way,' she conceded, 'but it is changing, slowly. Anyway, men can be possessive, too!'

'I don't understand that, either. I value my freedom far too much to want to restrict someone else's!'

'Have you ever been in love, really in love?'

'Once,' he said briefly. 'I thought I was, anyway!'

'What was she like?'

'Oh, just a girl. Local, she was.'

'What went wrong?'

'It was just like I said. When I was at college she moaned because we never had any money to go anywhere, or that I spent too much time working and not enough with her, and all her friends were getting engaged and why didn't we. It was awful!'

'And since then, there's been no one?'

'Not really. A few girls, but you know what it's like. You start talking and you find they've got nothing to say, or you've got nothing in common. I probably bore them, too. Anyway, there was never anyone I wanted to see more of.'

Annabel raised her eyebrows.

'Till you,' he added hastily. 'Don't fish, Annie. I hate all that kind of phoney stuff, anyway. I can't understand why it means so much to women, when they know it's just a line half the time. I don't say things I don't mean. You know you're a good-looking woman; why do you need me to tell you again?'

Annabel burst out laughing. He was honest, at least, and in a world of meaningless 'darlings' and insincere compliments, that was refreshing. If she was going to get involved with this man, it was obviously going to be on his terms, rather than hers.

'What are you laughing at?'

'It's just ... that you seem such an unlikely person to be in this business, somehow.'

A couple of teenagers wandered past with a transistor radio blaring. Annabel heard the announcer say, 'And now for a time-check; it's fourteen minutes to three.'

She jumped to her feet. 'Quarter to three! Suzy will wonder where I've got to. Richard, I'll have to be getting back.'

He stood up too. 'Did she know you were seeing me?'

Annabel flushed. 'No. I didn't say. It's such a small world and I hate the idea of a lot of gossip about me. Besides, there's Leonard. I don't want anyone to think that I'm just ... that I don't ...'

He smiled down at her. 'That's OK with me, Annie. I keep myself to myself anyway.'

They were standing very close together. She could see a little pulse beating in his neck. He kissed her. His lips were cool and undemanding at first, his tongue exploring gently. He tasted of summer. For a brief moment, he held her tight. Annabel's skin tingled, and she knew beyond doubt or guilt or questioning that they would make love, soon. They walked across the park, holding hands.

'Will you catch the Tube?'

'I'd better get a cab, since it's so late.'

'When will I see you again?'

'Lunchtime tomorrow?' It couldn't be too soon, for her.

'I think that's all right. I'll call you this evening anyway, just in case anything comes up and I can't make it.' They kissed again, in a desperate, clinging sort of way, in the shadow of Admiralty Arch. She twisted her fingers in his hair, wanting to be closer to him.

'This is crazy,' she murmured, surfacing. 'We're meeting again tomorrow!'

'Mmm,' said Richard, kissing her again, hungrily.

In the end he hailed a cab for her, and she twisted round in the seat to watch him until the cab turned the corner into Pall Mall and she couldn't see him any more. Then she took a deep breath and sat back. It was starting, it was all happening, just the way she had dreamed. She felt reckless and free. Even if it doesn't last for ever, isn't it worth having? She shivered slightly, remembering his kisses, his arms round her. Just physical attraction? No, the quality of 'difference' that had struck her right at the beginning was still there, and Annabel was always attracted to the unusual in men. What was it he had called himself? A weirdo? She chuckled as she took her mirror out and attempted to repair her make-up and hair. Was it her imagination or did her mouth really look so ... well, kissed? There were bright spots of colour on her cheeks and her eyes were shining. Naughtiness is good for me, obviously, she thought, exhilarated, as she tried to pull a comb through her windblown hair.

7

Leonard saw the change in Annabel immediately, and welcomed it, though not without a touch of regret that there didn't seem to be anything he himself could do to make her smile again. Still, she *was* smiling, and he was quietly glad for her. She was his laughing companion again, the girl who had so enchanted him when they first met, and her gaiety was so infectious that he simply counted his blessings, without ever questioning her. She was coming to see him regularly again; welcoming his telephone calls, brightening his life, making his rather sombre flat ring with her laughter. He couldn't, and didn't, complain.

It was Jacqui, returning from Los Angeles, who noticed the change most.

'My God!' she said, when Annabel met her at the airport, having driven Jacqui's mother, the au pair, and the children over to Heathrow in Ben's Range Rover.

'What's up?' Annabel laughed, while Joe clung to his mother's legs and Ben flung baby Alice high up in the air, producing delighted squeals from his daughter and tut-tuttings from the cautious Marie-Claude.

'You look fantastic, Annie! Did you manage to get away on holiday, then?'

Annabel flushed and Jacqui gave her a curious look.

'Er ... no, I didn't.'

'Well, something is obviously agreeing with you. You looked like a limp rag when I went away, and now you're blooming!'

Ben came over, his small daughter in his arms, and gave Annabel a kiss. 'What's happened, Annie? You look like the cat that's got the cream!'

But Annabel refused to be drawn. Not even to her oldest and dearest friends did she want to talk about this amazing, fantastic, bewildering thing that had happened to her. Annabel Lee was in love, fathoms deep in it, dizzy and exhilarated with it, and at the moment it was too new and precious a feeling to share with anyone.

Richard. *Richard*, she thought to herself, hugging the name to her. How was it possible to have got so involved so quickly? She was used to weighing up the possible consequences of any involvement, yet this time she was utterly content to be living for the moment.

Richard. He called her every day and they had long, foolish conversations about everything and nothing, inventing private jokes and a secret language of their own, like a couple of schoolchildren.

Richard. They met for lunch in quiet pubs full of sober-suited businessmen who looked askance at them as they held hands over the scarred wooden tables, and forgot to order anything to eat.

Richard. It hurt when she had to leave him to go back to the office while he went to the studio. They would catch the Underground together, feeling like conspirators, their fingers linked, hating the clock for taking them away from each other.

Richard. The way his hair curled at the back of his neck, his brown throat in an open-necked shirt. His unexpected tenderness; kissing the insides of her wrists, stroking her hair, smiling the little crooked smile that was so essentially him. With her, he had almost lost that air of detached watchfulness that had intrigued her so much at first. Almost, but not quite. As she came to know him better, she realized that he was the most liberated spirit she had ever known. All her other men friends had their vanities, their masculine pride, their touch of machismo, but not Richard. He told her, simply, that he didn't care what other people thought of him and in his case it was quite literally true. Most of the people Annabel knew, when they said that, were only concerned that they should be thought unconventional, arty or interesting. Richard honestly didn't care. He made no concessions, no attempt to be 'one of the lads'. If people got the wrong idea about him, he shrugged it off with a 'So what?' He fascinated Annabel.

One Saturday they were sitting on the grass in the middle of Regent's Park. Richard lay on his stomach, chewing a long grass stem. Annabel had gone past the stage when she felt she had to make conversation. Simply being beside him was enough. Suddenly she shivered and he sat up at once.

'Are you cold?'

'No, not really. It's just that the sun isn't as warm as it was.'

He put his arm round her and she lifted her face to his. He kissed her, and she felt her body stir. It was becoming more and more frustrating, this love-affair that wasn't. His kisses awoke a yearning response in her, and yet he never asked to come home with her. Sometimes, in secluded corners of parks or dimly-lit evening alleyways they would hold each other close and kiss until her mouth felt sore and bruised and her body fitted longingly into his ... and yet they both seemed to hesitate to go beyond that. He could hardly invite her home to his parents' house in Hackney, so it seemed as if the first move would have to come from her, and she felt shy about any blatant attempt at seduction. Besides, more often than not, Cindi was at Annabel's flat and, good friend though she was, Annabel knew that she would want to hear all about it afterwards, and her natural fastidiousness recoiled. Cindi was a child of her West Coast, Californian culture; Annabel still had a lot of inhibitions about sharing her love life with her friends. And, she discovered, she was still something of a romantic. She wanted the first time with Richard to be special, not just a quick tumble at the flat before Cindi came home. She wanted to sleep with him, using that much-misused phrase in its literal sense for once. If she couldn't have him for a whole night, she didn't want him at all.

She spent a couple of evenings each week with Leonard still, chatting to him about the agency and its ups and downs, allowing herself to be petted and spoiled as she had always been. Richard never indulged her, never gave her expensive presents, never looked at her with the devotion she saw in Leonard's eyes.

'I'm off to Edinburgh next week for a conference,' he told her one evening.

'Fun? Or just a bore?'

He laughed. 'Well, nothing special. Actually, Annie, I was wondering if you'd like to come with me? Hugo Carteret, my contact up there, is a very nice chap and has offered to put me up, and my guest, as he put it!'

Annabel shook her head and tried not to notice his crestfallen face. 'Not my scene, love. How long will you be away?'

'Wednesday till Friday or Saturday, I believe.'

Annabel's heart missed a beat. Cindi had told her only that morning that her schedule was taking her out of the country at the same time. No Cindi at the flat, no Leonard to telephone her ...

'Have a good time, then, love, and I'll see you when you get back!'

She called Richard after work the following evening. 'I'm going to have several free evenings next week. I thought we might go to the theatre, if you're free too. Wednesday, perhaps?'

'I'd like that. I enjoy the theatre, but I hardly ever get round to going except when I take my mum for her birthday treat!'

'Is there anything special you fancy seeing?'

'I've no idea what's on. It's ages since I looked at a paper!'

'How about that new rock musical? It got great reviews!'

'That sounds fine. I'm easy to please, Annie. I'll go and see anything!'

'I'll get some tickets then, shall I?'

They arranged to meet in a bar near the theatre half an hour before the performance started. It had been a dreary, grey day, and a steady drizzle was beginning to fall as Annabel drove home from work to get ready. She had a shower and washed her hair, and then wandered aimlessly round the flat, plumping up cushions, throwing dead flowers away, straightening books on the shelves, putting LPs back in their sleeves. What am I doing this for? she asked herself. Richard isn't going to be concerned about my housekeeping, for heaven's sake.

It was difficult to visualize him in the flat at all and if she tried to imagine making love with him her mind blanked out completely. The more she thought of it, the more she wondered how she had ever managed to go to bed with Malcolm; but then, at seventeen, she had been too dazzled to do anything but follow blindly where he led. And since then ... nothing. Oh, she had had plenty of propositions from people like Louis, but nothing she could take seriously. Whenever she had met anyone attractive and been even slightly tempted to get involved, there had always been the memory of Malcolm to pull her back; his absolute indifference and lack of interest in her once he'd got what he wanted and her own bitter hurt and disillusionment. There were too many men like Malcolm. It was no wonder she was cool towards them; ignoring their reasoned arguments, fending off their groping hands. With Leonard she felt safe, because Leonard belonged to a generation who respected their women. If, sometimes, she felt it was sad that passion couldn't be combined with that same respect, she accepted that that was the way life was.

But now there was Richard, and her stomach fluttered uncertainly at the thought of spending the night with him. He wouldn't abandon her, like Malcolm, or put her on a pedestal, like Leonard, but what would he do? Supposing he wasn't interested, didn't want her?

When they came out of the theatre, the half-hearted drizzle had turned into a steady downpour.

'Look at that!' said Annabel, disgusted.

'Where are you parked?'

'Not far away; I was lucky. Maybe I could make a dash for it.'

He peered up at the sky. 'You'd get soaked. Let's go and have some coffee across the road.'

There was a small Italian snackbar on the other side of the street. Richard ordered two cappucinos and brought them to a table. 'It was good, wasn't it?'

'Great! That chap, what's his name, who played the lead has so much personality. I nearly always enjoy the theatre, though, whatever's on. There's something about the atmosphere ...' She realized that she was rambling, and stole a glance at him. He sat at the other side of the table, sipping his coffee. He seemed like a stranger, a casual acquaintance at best. She couldn't do it. Yes, she could. If she let this chance go by it would be more nerve-racking next time. She wondered, briefly, how other people managed. It always seemed so easy to be a femme fatale. Eyes flashing messages, unspoken promises, a key slipped discreetly into a willing hand, never this shy and stumbling honesty. She took a deep breath.

'Richard!'

'Yes?'

'Would you like to – why don't you come back to my place?'

'That would be nice,' he said politely.

She was stammering like a schoolgirl. 'I mean ... only if

you want ... you don't have to.'

He reached across the table and took both her hands in his. 'Of course I want to.'

They smiled at each other.

'Come on, Annie, let's go.'

The rain had lessened slightly, but they were still damp when they reached Annabel's car and got in.

'Where's your van?' she asked him.

'I left it at the studio. It's so hard to park round here.'

They drove towards Annabel's flat in silence.

She opened the door. 'Welcome to the stately home,' she said flippantly, taut with nervousness. The hall was pine-panelled, with a set of Chinese prints that Leonard had brought back for Annabel from one of his trips abroad.

'Nice place!' said Richard appreciatively, looking round.

'Yes, we're quite happy with it.'

They went into the living-room, which looked unnaturally tidy after Annabel's attempts at clearing up. She switched on the spotlights which lit the shelves where the stereo was, and the corner which Cindi had crammed with potted plants. There were no chairs, only a corduroy corner-unit and a couple of sag-bags. The floor was polished wood, with brightly-coloured Indian durries and Annabel's favourite cream fur rug. The general effect was modern, tasteful – and homely.

'Isn't your flatmate in?'

'No, she's on a flight to Seattle this week.'

'That sounds nice,' he said enviously.

Silence fell again.

'Want some more coffee?'

'Please.'

She went into the kitchen and switched the percolator on. When she put her head round the living-room door again, he was on his knees looking through her record collection.

'Would you like something to eat?'

'Why not? What have you got?'

75

'Not a lot, actually. We could have some toast and honey?'

'Toast and honey it is.'

She brought the food in on a tray and sat on the floor to eat it. Once, she caught his eye, and smiled nervously, trying to ignore the leap of her heart.

'Shall I put some music on?'

'Sure, something nice and soothing.'

Annabel selected a James Taylor album. It began to play softly. Richard finished his toast and put the plate down. Automatically, she began to stack the plates on the tray, and got up to take them into the kitchen.

'Leave those just now.'

He held out his arms to her. His mouth was gentle and he tasted of coffee. They kissed, lingeringly, their arms round each other, more like friends than potential lovers. Annabel was frightened at her lack of response. Always, before, the touch of his lips had aroused her. On other occasions – at the barbecue, or kissing him in the park – she had felt an urgent, physical need. And now that she was alone with him, free from any possibility of interruption, she could feel nothing.

It's so easy for other people, she thought, panic-stricken. She had heard girls talking of their adventures, love-making no more to them than an evening's entertainment, strangers tumbling into bed like puppies with no thought of tomorrow, and nothing but a polite goodbye the next day.

She remembered Malcolm; his hard, cruel body, his cold eyes as she strove to please him, to do what he expected, to be as accomplished a lover as his more experienced partners. Abruptly, she stood up and moved away from him, into the middle of the room.

'What's the matter, Annie?'

She shook her head. Suddenly, he took a step towards her and buried his face in her hair.

'Oh, love, you smell so good!' His voice was husky. He raised his head and met her frightened eyes. 'Annie, it's been so long since I –'

'Sssh.' Her finger against his lips. 'For me, too. It's all right. It doesn't matter.'

'I don't think I could bear to disappoint you!'

She was incredulous. 'Disappoint me?' She realized, with a shock, that he was assuming her to be much more experienced than she was. She laughed gently. 'I've only ever ... there's only ever been one other man!'

He looked deep into her eyes. 'Then I'm very privileged!' he said quietly.

They kissed again, and touched each other, wonderingly. Somewhere, deep within her, Annabel felt the first unmistakable, welcome stirrings of desire. He undressed her with an awkward gentleness that she found infinitely touching. She saw that his hands were shaking and held them, for a moment, against her breasts, so that he could feel the beating of her heart. For the first time in her whole life Annabel was fiercely glad she was beautiful, proud of the pleasure her body could give him.

She took his shirt off and ran her fingertips lightly over his chest. Her fears melted away as the last of her clothes fell to the floor. He kissed her eyes and her throat and her breasts and as his lips travelled down her body she caught her breath and closed her eyes. It was all too much to bear ...

'You're beautiful ... Richard ...' Her voice sounded thick and strange, as if she were drunk, or drugged. Her legs seemed to dissolve and she was aware of the fur rug, soft against her bare flesh. 'Oh, yes ...' she said, 'yes ...'

There could be so much tenderness. Why did nobody ever mention the tenderness? The whispered words, the strokings and nibblings of love, the thrill of skin against bare skin, the salty taste of him against her lips, the unexpected softness behind his ears and in the corners of his mouth and the crook of his elbow, as she explored his body, delightedly, with her fingers and her tongue ... oh, why did no one say it could be like this ...

At first, she was very conscious of his restraint. She felt

77

him holding back, careful to carry her with him. But then he was moving over her and around her and inside her and somehow she seemed to be in another place, where there was no more thinking, but only feeling, and the sensation was concentrated into one tiny point. The point became a ripple, and then a series of ripples that washed over her whole body, and the ripples became waves, and at last there was just one glorious wave that was more powerful, more irresistible than anything she had ever imagined, and it made her sob and cling to him and cry out his name.

And afterwards, no real need for words, just warm arms around her and her mouth against his neck. How foolish and meaningless her fears seemed, now, set against the growing feeling that this was the way it should always be. Experience didn't matter, nervousness didn't matter, she realized joyfully, because what they had was something a dozen technique manuals or a thousand nights with strangers couldn't have taught them. A little loving.

He raised his head and smiled at her. 'Nice?'

'You know.'

'Oh, Annie.' He kissed her, luxuriantly.

'Mmmm.'

'What does that mean, mmm?'

'Just ... mmmm!'

He chuckled, and rolled over on to his side. 'Nice rug you've got here,' he teased. 'Polar bear, is it?'

She sat up, and stretched. 'I've no idea what it's made of, I just like it!' And I'll never be able to walk on it or look at it again without thinking about tonight, she told herself silently. 'I feel wonderful,' she said.

'I'm glad,' he said, simply.

'Do you want some more coffee, or shall we go to bed?'

'Is there any more coffee?'

'I think so.'

She went into the kitchen and poured two more cups.

They sat companionably on the living-room floor, drinking it, and giggling as Annabel tried to pull her towelling bath-robe around them both. For there could be laughter in love, too, and that was something else that Annabel had never expected. Later, when they were in bed, there was more laughter, and teasing, and silly jokes, and games when he pretended to bite her and she pretended to be frightened of him.

'Your toes are frozen!' Rolling over on to her again.

'Yours aren't too warm, either!'

Smiling, teasing, looking down at her tenderly until his eyes darkened with passion, and closed, and he came into her again, and the lovely movement began, the dip and sway and the beautiful, unbearable feeling that she was drowning ... or he was drowning ... and the small, lost cry ... was it his, or hers?

It didn't matter. Nothing mattered any more.

'Annie?'

'Mmmm?'

'I can't possibly tell you –'

She stopped his mouth with a kiss. 'Don't. There's no need.

He was silent for a while and Annabel thought he had fallen asleep, when he suddenly said, 'Annie?'

'Yes?'

'I bet you never thought we'd end up like this when you first met me at that barbecue, did you?'

'Did you?'

'No, not really. I thought you were really friendly, and intelligent, too. Someone I could talk to. I find I get bored with most women pretty quick, but not you.'

'That's nice to hear.'

'What did you think of me? When we first met, I mean?'

Annabel chuckled. 'Fancied you something rotten, didn't I?'

'Really?'

'Oh, Richard, you are absurd! Of course I did! Didn't you notice?'

He shook his head, bewildered, and she snuggled into his arms. 'It wasn't just that, though. I thought you were interesting, and a bit different from the usual crowd.'

He yawned suddenly. 'I'm tired!'

'Me, too.' She kissed him. 'Sleep, then.'

He fell asleep quickly, with his arms round her. Annabel found it hard to sleep herself. She was content to lie beside him, watching the quiet rhythm of his sleep, and feeling rich, and wise, and quite unbelievably happy.

8

Annabel woke at dawn. Always a light sleeper, she was aware of the unaccustomed presence of another person beside her before she was fully conscious. Richard slept as soundly as a child, one arm flung carelessly across her body. She turned round slightly, careful not to wake him, so that she could watch him sleep.

He's mine, she thought exultantly. For now, at any rate. Softly, very softly, she pressed her lips to his hair. He stirred, and murmured in his sleep. She smiled to herself and drew away, noting every detail of his face: the tiny wrinkle between his eyebrows, the faint dusting of freckles across the bridge of his nose, the way his lips were parted slightly as he slept.

I'll never, ever forget this, she thought gratefully. It wasn't just the love-making, fulfilling though that had been. It was this part too, the next morning, the testing time. She felt no doubt or fear or regret, no pangs of guilt; just gladness and the joyful certainty that whatever happened, she had done the right thing. She moved closer to him, and slept again.

He woke her with a kiss.

'Mmmm? What?' she murmured, surfacing.

He laughed softly. 'I said morning, missus!'

They smiled at each other.

'What time is it?' she asked him, groping on her bedside table for her alarm clock.

'Just after eight. Time I was getting up!'

'Do you have to?' she said, pressing her body to his, aware

of his instant response. He bent his head and ran his tongue around her left nipple teasingly.

'Don't tempt me, Annie. I've got to go to work!'

She sighed. 'OK, I know, so have I. I'll get some breakfast.'

She scrambled out of bed and made her way, a bit groggily, into the kitchen. She poured herself a glassful of cold orange juice, which made her feel slightly more alive. Her body felt stretched and sore, and she grinned unrepentantly to herself as she remembered exactly why! Richard came into the kitchen, yawning, wearing nothing but his jeans, and she poured him some orange juice too. She put instant coffee into two mugs, and switched the toaster on.

'How do you feel?' he asked her.

'A bit tired, but otherwise, fantastic!' she assured him. He kissed the back of her neck. She twisted round to face him, her arms round his neck.

'Oh, Richard ...' She paused. She had been going to say, 'I love you,' but something held her back. Would he think she was clinging, pushing him into some kind of commitment, assuming that making love with him gave her some sort of hold over him? Instinct told her that that wasn't the way to hold a man like Richard. If he felt he was free to go, he would probably return. Besides, he hadn't said he loved her, and she still had some pride left. She released him with a laugh. 'Mustn't let the toast burn, this is the last of the bread!'

They sat with the morning papers and the Breakfast Show on the radio, like an old married couple.

'What time do you get into the studio, as a rule?'

'It depends. Sometimes nine, sometimes ten. I want to be early this morning, though; we've got a session.'

'Do you want me to give you a lift?'

'No, no, I'll get the Tube!'

'Sure?'

'Of course.'

At the front door he paused for a moment, and put his arms round her. 'I'll call you this evening, OK?'

'Fine.'

'Right, then.'

They smiled at each other.

'Annie?'

'Yes?'

'I just want to say ... thank you.'

She was suddenly inexpressibly moved, and her eyes filled with tears. She shook her head, unable to speak.

'What is it, love? You're crying!'

'It's nothing. I –'

'You're not sorry?'

'Oh, no, no, nothing like that. I don't know why I'm crying. Maybe I just don't want you to go. Or something. I don't know.'

He looked uncertain. 'Well, look, I've got to go. I'll be late for the session!'

She gave him a little push, half-laughing through her tears. 'Go on then, off you go!'

He squeezed her hand once and then left. Annabel wondered why she felt so desolate and told herself it was just lack of sleep, coupled with an emotional reaction to the events of the past twenty-four hours.

Suzy was on the telephone when she got into the office, hiding once again behind dark glasses.

'Morning, Annie!' she said, when she had put the phone down.

'Morning. Was that anything important?'

'*Woman's Choice* want to put a provisional booking on Dominique for Friday. It's their autumn fashion round-up so it should be around six pages.'

'Sounds OK. When will they confirm?'

'This afternoon, most probably.'

Gillian brought in some coffee and Annabel sipped it gratefully.

'Did you have a nice evening? How was the theatre?'

'Oh, great! The critics were spot-on for once; it's a really good show,' said Annabel, after a pause. Going to the theatre with Richard seemed a million light years ago. She had simply told Suzy she was going with a friend. It does make a difference, making love, she thought suddenly, whatever anyone says. I've got nothing more to offer him, now. Supposing he doesn't ring me this evening ...

He did ring, though. 'Hello there.'

She felt weak with relief. 'Hello. How are you?'

'Sleepy!'

She giggled. 'Me, too. Are you working late tonight?'

'Yes, unfortunately. I've got a session of my own until ten.'

'Pity. I thought we might meet ...'

'Sorry, love, I can't. I'll see you soon, though. Tomorrow lunch-time?'

She flipped through the pages of her diary, knowing that even if she did have an appointment she would change it, or postpone it, or even get Gillian to phone through and say she was ill. She needed to see him again, to reassure herself that everything was the same as it had always been. No, not the same, better.

The following day's lunch-hour was a blank.

'Yes, OK, I'll see you then. Ciao!'

'What's that?'

'Ciao. It's Italian, for goodbye!'

'You don't say. Cor blimey,' he said, deadpan, deliberately accentuating his Cockney intonation.

'You're crazy!'

'But you love me just the same, don't you?' he said flippantly. She didn't reply, feeling that anything she said would give her away.

'Till tomorrow, then. Take care!'

'Bye!'

It was going to be all right. It had to be. When they met the next day she was reassured. He treated her in exactly the same way as he had always done: affectionate, laconic, saying what he thought but almost never what he felt. She longed to ask him if he loved her, but she refused to give in to the temptation. He had once told her that part of her attraction for him was her independent spirit, the fact that she didn't wheedle and cling like other girls; and Annabel, who had always been so proud of her independence, now found herself trapped by it.

Not that she was unhappy. She knew he cared about her; he called her every day and saw her as often as his work schedule, and hers, allowed. Sometimes it was simply a snatched hour at lunch time or after work. Occasionally they met at weekends, but as he worked harder and harder to establish himself as a photographer, he spent more and more Saturdays in the studio. They had very few chances to spend complete nights together but sometimes, as they sat in the park at lunchtime, kissing and whispering, their bodies would move together involuntarily and he would murmur against her hair, 'Have we got time to go over to your place? Is Cindi in?' and Annabel found that their love-making was no less sweet for being stolen, after all.

But still, there was Leonard. Annabel saw him regularly and outwardly their relationship had not changed. Increasingly, though, she felt she was playing a part, being the Annabel Lee Leonard expected her to be, instead of being natural. How can he not suspect, she thought; he knows me so well. The idea that he might choose not to suspect, preferring to let her affair with Richard run its course and hope she would return to him in the end, never occurred to her. It's no good, she thought as she was changing to go out to dinner with him one evening. I'll have to tell him. It isn't fair to him to go on like this.

One evening, he took her out to dinner at a country pub in Hertfordshire, and as he gave his order to the waiter, she sat biting her lip and wondering how she could introduce the subject of Richard. While she was eating her quiche, Leonard gave her the opportunity, unknowingly, by mentioning that there was a play in the West End that he would like to see.

'It isn't often I fancy going to the theatre,' he said, reaching for her hand across the table, 'and I know you enjoy it, don't you? Poor Annie, you miss out on all this culture seeing so much of me!'

Annabel took a deep breath. 'Well, I do sometimes get the chance to go while you're away,' she said. 'As a matter of fact, when you were up in Edinburgh I went to see that new rock musical –'

'Doesn't sound like my cup of tea, a rock musical,' he said easily. 'Give me a nice Gilbert and Sullivan any day, something with a bit of a tune! I did go and see that hippy thing, what was its name ...'

'Hair,' said Annabel automatically.

'Oh, yes, Hair. Well, I must say I thought it was horrible. All that leaping and gyrating about they seem to call dancing these days, and the music was so loud! It's not for me. Still, each to his own, eh, Annie? It would be a dull old world if we all liked the same things!'

'Yes,' said Annabel blankly. Then she tried again. 'I went with Ben Lawrence's assistant.'

'Oh, yes, the David Bailey type? Nice chap, is he?'

At that moment the steaks arrived, and by the time they had been served, and the waiter had brought Leonard's green beans and broccoli and a mixed salad for Annabel, the moment had passed.

Annabel ate her steak mechanically, her mind racing. It really did seem as if Leonard was doing his best not to be told; or was she being over-sensitive? They finished their meal, coffee and brandy were served, and Annabel waited for another opportunity to mention Richard. It never came. Besides, what can I say? she asked herself helplessly.

'Penny for your thoughts?' said Leonard, gently.

She smiled at him and shook her head. 'They're not worth a penny!'

He looked at her with such open devotion that she felt a rush of tenderness for him. I can't tell him, or not now, she thought, and it's not just because I don't want to hurt him. I don't want to lose him, either! Heaven help me, I do love him, in a way. It's not like the way I love Richard, but I can't imagine life without Leonard, either! Can I possibly be in love with two men at once?

'I wanted to ask you a favour, actually,' he said, suddenly.

'Me?' Annabel was genuinely surprised. She realized, with a sudden shock, that he hardly ever asked her for anything, though he gave her so much.

He laughed. 'Don't look so astonished!'

'Well, what is it? You know I'll do it if I can!'

'I'm giving a dinner-party at the end of next week for some colleagues and some friends, at my place. I'd like you to act as hostess, if you don't mind.'

Annabel was flattered. 'Leonard, of course I will!'

'There won't be that much to do. Mrs Elliott has told me that she can cope with the cooking, so it's just – well, to tell you the truth, Annie, I don't want to be a typical crusty old bachelor entertaining on his own!'

'Oh, Leonard! As if anyone thinks of you that way!'

He seemed so delighted at her response that Annabel felt even more confused. Leonard really wanted her to be part of his life; with Richard, she fitted in where she could. He had never suggested taking her to meet his family, though she asked eager questions about them when they met. She forgot, briefly, that it was she who had insisted they keep their relationship secret. Settling into the passenger seat of Leonard's luxurious car, she thought for a moment that it was nice to *know* she came first with Leonard, before his work or his ambitions or anything else. She turned to smile gratefully at him. He is good to me, she thought. Yet her heart didn't turn over when she saw him making his way across a crowded bar towards her, her knees didn't turn to water when he kissed her, she didn't yearn to have him by her side for always, as she did with Richard. It was all very confusing.

She needed to talk to someone. Someone level-headed and sensible, who would straighten it all out for her. Jacqui, really her closest friend, was the obvious person, but Annabel hesitated. It wasn't just that Richard worked with Ben and Jacqui knew him well. It was also because her friend was, deep down, a very conventional lady, and Annabel wasn't at all sure she'd understand. Jacqui, with her secure, happy family life; Jacqui, who had married Ben at nineteen and, Annabel was sure, not so much as looked at another man since then; no, she couldn't tell Jacqui. Suzy admired Leonard too much, and she was in the business too. It could be embarrassing. Annabel had seen it happen before.

Which left Cindi, and the more Annabel thought about her the more she wondered why she hadn't confided in her before. Cool, Californian Cindi, who had been 'heavy into consciousness-raising', as she put it, ever since she was in High School. Cindi wouldn't think it strange that Annabel seemed to be in love with two men.

One night, over a bottle of plonk in the flat, she confessed. Cindi's reaction was just what she thought it might be.

'So what's your problem?' she said, wrinkling her tanned nose.

'Well ... *can* I be in love with them both? They're so different!'

'So who says love always has to be the same? There's no blueprint, you know, Annie!'

'You think it's possible, then?'

Cindi laughed. 'Well, you should know. They're your feelings! If you feel love for Leonard ...'

'I'm not sure that it's love, but I do feel great affection, and I'd feel terrible if I knew I was never going to see him again!'

'And this other guy, this what's-his-name ...'

'Richard.'

Cindi looked at her friend sharply. Annabel's face had softened, her eyes glowed, her mouth curved into a smile.

'Oh, wow, now that looks like the real McCoy!' she laughed.

Annabel laughed too, a bit defensively. 'He's very ... special,' she said quietly. Cindi waited.

'Do you think I should tell Leonard? I tried to, but he –'

Cindi stared at her in amazement. '*Tell* him? Tell him what?'

'Well, about Richard.'

'*What* about Richard?'

'That I ... love him. That we're sleeping together.'

'Now I know you're crazy,' said Cindi. 'What earthly good do you imagine it would do to tell that nice guy that?'

'But I feel so guilty –'

'Aha!' Cindi pounced on her words like a prosecuting counsel.

'*You* feel guilty. And because you feel bad about it, you want to unload your guilt on to poor Leonard, just to make yourself feel better. And you say you love him. That's a weird kind of love, Annie! You don't want to hurt Leonard, so you keep quiet. That way he's happy, Richard's happy, and you're happy, apart from that old-fashioned British conscience that says you should tell all. Is anyone going to be any happier if you do 'fess up?'

'No,' said Annabel, smiling in spite of herself.

'Well, then, just let things take their course!'

When Richard telephoned her in the office the next day she was halfway through interviewing a sixteen-year-old who was very keen to become a model.

'Excuse me,' she said politely, as she heard Richard's voice on the other end of the line.

'Annie? It's me!'

'Listen, can you call me at home tonight, love? I'm a bit tied up at the moment interviewing a new lady.'

'OK, Miss Lee. I just wanted to tell you I'm going on a trip to Tunisia next week. My first ever trip abroad!'

'Oh, that's marvellous! I'll talk to you tonight, love!'

9

Richard phoned Annabel from Heathrow before he left for Tunisia. 'Just to say goodbye!' he said, sounding cheerful. A lump seemed to have appeared in Annabel's throat.

'Have a good time, love. I'll miss you!'

'I'll miss you too, Annie – but here's some good news. Ben's offered to make me a partner in the studio and get another assistant!'

Annabel gasped. 'Richard, I'm so pleased for you! That's fantastic!'

The pips went.

'Take care, then!'

'I will. See you next week, love!'

To cheer herself up, Annabel went out and treated herself to a dark-blue straight-skirted dress, slit to the thighs, to wear for Leonard's dinner-party.

On Friday she felt surprisingly nervous as she drove over towards St John's Wood. It was the first time Leonard had specifically asked her to act as his hostess. Maybe she was reading too much into the gesture ...

He opened the flat door just as she was rummaging for her key.

'Come in, Annabel. You look wonderful!' He kissed her on the cheek.

'Hello, love,' she said. 'Is everything OK?'

'Yes, fine. Mrs Elliott has got some help in the kitchen, so there's nothing for you to do except make conversation. And look beautiful – which you do!' he added, smiling at her.

'Who's coming, again?' Annabel asked, helping herself to some salted peanuts from a silver dish.

'Well, you know Joe and Irene Tilman, my old friends.'

Annabel nodded.

'Hugo Carteret, my colleague from the Edinburgh branch, and his wife. Sheila Monroe is our Sales Director here in London, and I invited the young chap I work with, Ian McLeod, to make up the numbers. He's not much more than your age, Annie; you'll like him!'

Annabel wondered briefly whether she really would. She'd noticed on previous occasions that Leonard tended to assume that anyone under thirty-five was automatically a kindred spirit. It didn't follow; she had more in common with Leonard than with most of the younger men she met.

She was sipping a Martini when the doorbell rang. Leonard went to answer it, and a few moments later he ushered a couple into the room.

'Annabel, this is my colleague Hugo Carteret, and his wife Marie. Hugo, Marie, this is Annabel Lee.'

'Delighted to meet you, my dear,' said Hugo Carteret. He was a tall, stooping, scholarly-looking man with a crest of iron-grey hair and a gentle Scottish accent. His wife was tiny, dark and quietly attractive, in a fussy green dress that didn't do anything for her figure.

'Hello,' she said, smiling shyly at Annabel, who smiled back.

'Let me get you a drink, Marie? Hugo?'

Marie Carteret blushed. 'I'm afraid we don't. Didn't Hugo mention ...'

'We're total abstainers,' said Hugo.

Well, now, thought Annabel in some amusement, there's a fun start to the evening.

'I have some fresh orange juice. Would you like some of that?' said Leonard valiantly. The Carterets agreed, and Leonard disappeared into the kitchen. There was an awkward silence.

'Are you down from Edinburgh for the weekend?' ventured Annabel.

'Part business, part pleasure,' said Hugo. 'I have some people to see next week, so we thought we'd make a wee break of it.'

'That's nice,' said Annabel brightly. 'I often think we Londoners take the place for granted. You'll be doing some sightseeing while you're here, I suppose?'

'Indeed I will. There are several City churches I haven't yet seen,' said Hugo enthusiastically.

'Hugo's an expert on Church architecture of the – what is it – eighteenth century,' said Leonard, coming into the room with two glasses of orange juice. 'He had a book on it published last year!'

'Really?' said Annabel, wondering if there was anything she could say about Church architecture, and deciding there wasn't.

She was profoundly relieved when the doorbell rang again and she heard Joe Tilman's booming voice in the hall. I never thought I'd see the day when I'd be delighted to see Joe and Irene walk into a room, she reflected. She turned to Joe with a beaming smile which he immediately misinterpreted.

'Annabel! Come here, you gorgeous creature, and give old Joe a bit of a cuddle!' he bellowed.

She went over to him and he kissed her full on the mouth with more enthusiasm than was strictly necessary.

'Mmmm. You're luscious!' he muttered, in a stage whisper. 'Don't forget, Annabel, when you get tired of Leonard you can always turn to your old friend Joe!'

'Don't get excited, Annabel. He says that to all the girls,' said Irene Tilman waspishly. 'One day one of these nubile young lovelies is going to take him at his word, and what will you do then, Joe?'

'I'd like you to meet Hugo and Marie Carteret,' said Leonard tactfully, to cover the awkward moment. Joe Tilman crushed Marie Carteret's fragile hand in his huge paw.

'Glad to meet you, m'dear. Scottish, eh? A braw Scots lassie?' He pinched her cheek and Marie recoiled, blushing.

'I think Joe's had two or three already,' muttered Leonard to Annabel.

The bell rang again, much to everyone's relief, while Annabel was wondering how to include both couples in conversation. Leonard's young colleague Ian McLeod was a pleasant-looking young man with a neat black beard, and Sheila Monroe, whom Annabel vaguely remembered having met before, was a tall, elegant brunette in her late forties, in a beautifully-cut linen two-piece. Leonard organized drinks all round, Hugo Carteret and Sheila Monroe began talking 'shop', and Annabel found herself pinned in a corner between Irene Tilman and Marie Carteret, who were soon deep in a discussion of the problems of bringing up teenagers.

When they went into the dining-room, even Annabel was impressed. Every speck of silver gleamed, from the cruet to the candle-holders, and the tablecloth and napkins were of the finest Irish linen. Somewhat to her dismay, she found herself sitting between Joe Tilman and Ian McLeod, with Sheila Monroe directly opposite.

'Mmmm, this is excellent,' said Joe Tilman, smacking his lips. 'I must say, Leonard old man, your Mrs Elliott is a first-rate cook. Looks after you better than a wife, eh? In some ways, anyway!'

There was a frozen silence.

'Certainly, I don't know where I'd be without her,' said Leonard equably. 'More soup, anyone?'

Annabel stifled a giggle. Joe's really outrageous, she thought. He annoys me sometimes but at least he's half alive, which is more than can be said for the rest of them. Still, I really should do my best to keep the conversation going ...

The sounds of spoons transferring soup from plates to lips

were embarrassingly loud in the silence. Before Annabel could say anything, Sheila Monroe spoke to her.

'How's the work going, Annabel?'

'Oh, very well, thanks,' she said, smiling. 'It keeps me busy, anyway!'

'Annabel is a fashion model,' Sheila informed the party.

'Actually, I run an agency,' Annabel put in quickly.

'Oh? Now why ... I could have sworn Leonard said you were a model!'

'I used to be, but I didn't like it, so I decided to run an agency instead. It suits me much better.'

'Modelling always seems like a rather degrading way to earn one's living to me,' said Sheila Monroe unexpectedly. 'All that parading around half-dressed, turning yourself into a sexual object for men to ogle at.'

'I do enjoy a good ogle,' said Joe Tilman.

'I don't think many models would see it like that,' said Annabel quietly. 'For a start, no girl has to do swimwear or underwear shots unless she wants to. My agency does no nude work, but even the girls who do that are perfectly willing, so I don't see that they're being exploited in any way. For a girl who looks good and can project a bit of personality in front of a camera, it's a pleasant way to earn good money. More fun than, say, typing, or working in a shop, anyway!'

'But don't you think that women today have more career choices than that?'

'Well, some do, obviously, but I don't see why making use of your natural good looks is any more degrading than making use of any other talent!' said Annabel.

'Hear, hear,' said Joe Tilman. 'Good for you, Annabel. Let's hear no more of this Women's Liberation nonsense. Out of the boardroom and into the bedroom with 'em, that's what I say!'

'Well, really!' Sheila looked genuinely offended, and Annabel smiled at her.

'Don't take any notice of him. He only talks like that for effect, don't you, Joe?'

'I never argue with a beautiful woman, let alone two beautiful women,' beamed Joe good-naturedly. 'You career girls have got to stick together, anyway.'

'Maybe he's right!' said Sheila Monroe, with more friendliness then she had previously shown Annabel.

I wonder if she fancies Leonard, Annabel thought, her perceptions heightened by a couple of glasses of wine. I bet she does and I bet she had me pinned down as some dumb dollybird who was keeping him amused! Now that she knows I've got my own business, it looks like she sees me as a worthy rival! The idea of competing with anyone for Leonard's affection was so bizarre that she almost laughed out loud. She glanced at him, deep in conversation with Hugo Carteret at the other end of the table. He *is* attractive, she thought; no wonder Sheila Monroe fancies her chances! The thought gave her no jealousy, just an amused interest. I'm smug about Leonard, she thought. It would serve me right if he did run off with Sheila Monroe! The idea of her conventional Leonard and the rather stately Miss Monroe 'running off' together made her smile to herself.

She was jerked back into reality by a hand creeping inexorably up her thigh. She sat frozen with shock for a moment until she saw the glazed expression in Joe Tilman's eyes. Oh, really, she thought angrily, this is too much! She managed to slide a small knife off the table and, under cover of the white linen tablecloth, jab it into the groping hand. Joe yelped, and hastily tried to cover up by clattering his plate around. Annabel pointedly moved her chair away. She saw Irene Tilman watching her from the other end of the table, and sighed inwardly. As dinner-parties go, she thought, this one was really hard work.

Mrs Elliott cleared away the plates and Leonard suggested that they go back into the living room for coffee. On the way, he came up to Annabel and whispered in her ear, 'How's it going, love?'

'Oh, not too badly.'

'Joe's had a few, hasn't he?'

'Well, you know Joe,' said Annabel, more tolerantly than she felt. Being an old friend of Leonard's didn't give him the right to behave as he had been doing. Over coffee, Irene Tilman proposed a rubber of bridge, and Annabel was tremendously thankful when first the Carterets and then Ian McLeod declined. I'm not up to this, she thought suddenly, these aren't my sort of people, I don't fit in. My idea of a dinner-party is sitting on the floor with a plate of spaghetti bolognese and a bottle of plonk and people I really like, not business friends I'm obliged to be polite to! This might be Leonard's world, but it isn't mine! Oh, Richard, where are you?

IO

Annabel was up early the next morning. Cindi, staggering out of bed at ten-thirty after a late flight that had got her into London in the small hours, found her prowling restlessly around the flat, unable to settle to any of her usual Saturday jobs.

'Whatever's the matter, Annie?' she asked, yawning. 'It makes me feel tired just looking at you!'

Annabel smiled rather vaguely. 'I'm all right, I was just thinking.'

'Have you had a tough week?'

'Not really, but it was Leonard's dinner-party last night.'

'Oh, of course, I forgot. How was it?'

Annabel looked thoughtful. 'It was ... a bit strange. A funny mix of people, I suppose. I felt as if I didn't really fit in.'

'Hmmm,' said Cindi. 'Are you missing Richard?'

'Well, yes. Yes, I am. I looked round at those people last night and ... I wanted him to be there.'

'You should sort it out with him, Annie!'

'But how can I? I knew all along how it would be. He's got his work and I've got mine, and there's Leonard, besides. He's part of my life and I'm part of his. I'm not part of Richard's – or only a tiny part.'

As she spoke, a thought occurred to Annabel. She knew where Richard lived; she'd seen letters addressed to him at Ben's studio. Speedwell Street, Hackney. She could take the car and be over there in fifteen minutes. He'd never exactly said he didn't want to take her home. She had asked eager questions about his house, his parents, his married brother, his sister who had run off with a married man and gone to live in Newcastle, anything to get to know more about the other, hidden side of his life.

It was no more than twenty minutes from the elegant Georgian terraces of Primrose Hill to the grimy streets of Hackney, but it could have been another world. The main roads were crammed with Saturday-morning shoppers; overweight middle-aged women with shopping trolleys, down-at-heel young mums with babies in prams and two or three other children clinging to their skirts, hollow-cheeked old men in flat caps and baggy trousers, Indian women like bright exotic birds in their saris, young blacks in jeans and dreadlocks. Annabel eased the MGB into a side street and checked with her A-Z. If she went right *here*, under the railway, and then took the second turning on the left ...

Speedwell Street turned out to be a street like a thousand others. Red-brick terraced houses with peeling paintwork and tiny, apologetic squares of dusty garden. Number Seven had a neat privet hedge and a blue front door. So that's Richard's home, Annabel thought, pulling up on the other side of the road and gazing in fascination.

She got out of the car and walked briskly up the street. There was a small general store on the corner. She went in, setting the doorbell jangling, and bought a jar of coffee that she didn't really want. It was a corner-shop of the old-fashioned kind, selling everything from shampoo and aspirins to broken biscuits in big glass-fronted tins.

It reminds me of old Ma Williams' shop back home, Annabel thought – and then she realized that the whole of Speedwell Street could have been transplanted to Nottingham and you wouldn't be able to see the difference. She left the shop, and looked both ways, along the rows of identical terraces. I've come round in a circle, she thought. I've been fighting for the last seven years to get away from streets like this!

I'd never fit in here either, she thought with sudden awareness. Not after all this time. I'd be out of place, just as out of place as I felt yesterday evening with Leonard's friends. Where *do* I belong?

The following Wednesday, Richard came back from Tunisia. Annabel was busy that day, so when he called she couldn't talk for long. He suggested a quick drink after work, so at six-thirty she drove over to the pub near Ben's studio. Her heart contracted when she saw Richard. A week in the sun had deepened his tan and streaked his hair blond. He flung his arms around her.

'Annie. It's good to see you!'

She buried her face against his shoulder, savouring the warm, faintly foreign smell of him.

'Oh, Richard, I missed you!'

'Did you?' he said, smiling. He ordered the drinks and then sat down beside her, stretching his long legs in front of him.

'How was it?

'I was pleased with the way it all went and I think the clients were too. The models were very easy to work with.'

'You enjoyed it then?'

'Yes. It was hard work, but going abroad makes me feel as if I'm getting somewhere at last. What with that, and this new deal I'm doing with Ben, things are really looking up!'

'The sky's the limit,' said Annabel, wondering why the thought gave her no pleasure. She wanted Richard to get on, of course she did. *Even if it takes him away from me?*

'How about you, Annie? What have you been doing?'

'Oh, nothing much. Leonard gave a dinner-party on Friday which was quite pleasant. Cindi was home over the weekend so I spent most of it with her. Nothing special's happened at work.'

At first, Annabel had felt self-conscious about mentioning Leonard's name in front of Richard, but as he had never shown any sign of jealousy, or indeed made any comment at all, she had stopped bothering about it. Richard had said he didn't want to take away her freedom, right at the start, and it seemed that he meant it. Of course, she had said the same, but she could sense that their relationship was changing imperceptibly. For one thing, there was a difference between an obscure assistant, even to someone as well-known and respected as Ben, and an in-demand fashion photographer. Oddly enough, that particular difference was brought home to Annabel sharply not long after Richard had returned from Tunisia.

She had had one of those days at the office. Suzy was off work with flu, which effectively doubled Annabel's workload. One of the lines on the office switchboard suddenly went on the blink and Gillian was kept occupied most of the morning chasing up the engineers. Claire Traynor overslept and was late for an important session. A client rang up insisting that he'd put a provisional booking on Britt, but Annabel could find no record of it and in the meantime Britt had been booked elsewhere. After the angry client had rung off, Annabel turned round sharply and knocked the remains of her cup of coffee over. She watched, mesmerized, as a pool of lukewarm coffee spread over the model cards she was sorting through. She mopped it up with tissues as best she could and then, on a sudden impulse, she picked up the phone and dialled Ben's studio.

'Yes?'

She recognized the voice of Fred, whom Ben had recently taken on as a kind of junior assistant to himself and Richard.

'Could I speak to Richard Redding, please?'

'He's working right now. Is it urgent?'

'Yes!'

'Who's calling?'

'Annabel Lee.'

She heard the clatter as he put the phone down and a few moments later she heard Richard's voice.

'What is it, Annabel?'

'Oh, Richard, I've had such a terrible day!'

There was a pause.

'Have you, love? I'm sorry!' he said kindly.

'Listen, can you meet me after work?'

'I'm working till ten tonight, Annie!'

Silence. Of course he's working; he can't just drop everything and come and comfort me. I shouldn't expect him to.

'Annabel? Are you still there?'

'Yes, I'm here.'

'Look, I'll call you after the session, OK?'

'OK.'

'You do understand, don't you?'

'Yes, I understand. It's all right.'

Slowly she put the telephone down. It's always going to be like this from now on, she thought with sudden insight. He'll be there, he'll talk to me, he'll call me ... when he's not too busy. I'm important to him, but his work is more important than me, more important than anything. I'm always going to come second, with Richard.

Later, when Gillian had gone home, she sat in the office by herself. I need him, I really need him, she thought. I needed him to be with me tonight, and he let me down. Love might hit you suddenly, like it did when I first met Richard, but need is insidious, creeping up on you when you least expect it. I've got no claims on Richard, nothing to offer him, no rights at all.

Instead of going home, she drove up to Hampstead and called in on Jacqui. Ben wasn't yet home, and Jacqui was just about to put the children to bed, with the help of Marie-Claude.

'Hello, Annie. What a nice surprise!'

'Yes, well, I thought I'd drop by. How's things?'

'I can't grumble,' said Jacqui, smiling. 'Two or three days' work a week seems to suit me fine; it gives me more time for these little horrors!' She put an arm round Joe as she spoke.

'Am I a horror, mummy?' he asked her, seriously.

'Sometimes, aren't you? When you're naughty?'

Joe grinned up at Annabel. 'Are you going to give me my bath, Annie?'

Jacqui had encouraged Joe to call Annabel 'Auntie' at first, but when Annabel protested that it made her feel like an ancient monument she had become simply Annie.

'Would you like me to?'

'Ooh, yes. I can show you my submarine!'

Sitting in the bathroom, with Joe's damp little body on her lap, she allowed herself to fantasize for a moment. Suppose she had children. She could still work, just as Jacqui did. She and Richard between them could earn more than enough to run a comfortable home and pay for help in the house. It was possible, people did it all the time.

But it's not what Richard wants, she told herself sternly. And you can't be certain it's what you want, either! Jacqui's an ideal mum. She was dreaming of a home and a family when you first met her; it's what she always wanted. Playing with Joe and Alice for half an hour at bath time isn't the same as having them around all the time.

'You look very thoughtful, Annie,' said Jacqui.

Annabel gave Joe and final hug and buttoned him into his pyjamas. 'I think I'm getting broody in my old age,' she said lightly.

Jacqui raised her eyebrows. 'Doesn't sound like you, love. You wouldn't want them if you'd had a day like I've just had!'

'You and me both!'

Jacqui was instantly sympathetic. 'Why, what happened?'

Annabel catalogued the day's disasters, without mentioning the final phone call to Richard.

'It may not sound much,' she finished, 'but it was just one thing after another and that's what did me in.'

'Oh, I know. I get days like that, when nothing goes right.

You should have given Leonard a call.'

'Well, but ... I don't always want to run to him when things go wrong. I'm supposed to be able to cope on my own!'

'Wherever did you get that idea?' said Jacqui, as she tucked little Alice into her cot. 'What are friends for, if not to take your troubles to? You don't want to get the idea there's anything wrong with showing a man that you need him!'

'But what if he doesn't need you?'

Jacqui looked at her, wide-eyed. 'Oh, Annie, how can you say that? Of course Leonard needs you! His eyes simply light up when you walk into a room! Don't tell me you hadn't noticed!'

Annabel was silent. It was on the tip of her tongue to tell Jacqui it wasn't Leonard she was thinking of, but someone else. *I don't have to tell her it's Richard, and it would be a relief to talk to her*, she thought.

'Aren't things going well between you and Leonard, Annie?'

Annabel took refuge in a half-truth. 'I've been wondering about it ever since that dinner-party he gave with the Tilmans and that dreary couple from Scotland. Oh – that's not fair, they weren't really dreary, it was just that ... I don't know, we didn't have anything at all in common and I felt like a fish out of water. They say that one of the signs of compatibility is whether you get on with each other's friends, don't they?'

Jacqui giggled. 'I don't know about that. When I first met Ben he only seemed to know a dreadful crowd of Welsh rugby fanatics who never seemed to do anything but get drunk and then recite awful rude poems when we went out with them. I'm sure they thought I was a terrible prude!'

'I believe I remember you and Ben fixing me up a blind date with one, just before I met Malcolm Roberts!' said Annabel.

'Oh, yes, that was Gareth,' said Jacqui, smiling. 'Actually he was one of the better ones, believe it or not. He's married now, to a very Welsh Welsh lady called Myfanwy.'

'That all seems a long time ago.'

'You mean Malcolm?'

'Well, yes, all the time when I was modelling. As for Malcolm, the rat, I hope he's ended up with someone as nasty as himself!'

'You sound bitter,' said Jacqui. 'Don't be, love. It doesn't do any good, and it *was* a long time ago.'

When Ben finally got home he hugged Jacqui, smiled at Annabel and flopped into a chair.

'I'll get you something to eat, darling,' said Jacqui, getting up.

Ben squeezed her hand gratefully as she went past him and Annabel felt suddenly left-out and lonely. Ben and Jacqui are all right, they've got each other, she thought. That's what I need: someone I can always depend on, someone who'll be my other half. Jacqui's so lucky; she never seemed to have any doubts about what – or who – she wanted. There was never anyone but Jacqui for Ben, either. If only it could be that simple for me. If only I could be sure that Leonard's world, or Richard's, was where I belong.

'How's things at work, Annie? OK?' asked Ben.

'Today wasn't too good. I had a row with a client and one or two other problems. Suzy's away, too, which doesn't help. She's much more efficient than I am, really.'

'It's very important to work with the right people,' Ben continued thoughtfully. 'I'd never have let Richard share my studio the way I did if I hadn't got on so well with him as a person. He's a great bloke!'

'Yes. Yes, he is nice,' said Annabel demurely. 'He's doing well, too, from what I hear.'

'He is indeed,' said Ben. 'Quite honestly I doubt he'll be around that much longer. I'm pretty sure the Americans will snap him up once he's done a bit more work here.'

Annabel looked at him, speechless for a moment. 'You think so?' she said at last.

'Sure to. There's so much money to be made in New York and it's prestige work, too. Richard's got no ties and I know he wants to travel.'

'Yes. He told me that once,' said Annabel.

She left Ben and Jacqui's at ten-thirty and drove slowly home. As she opened the front door she heard the sound of voices from the living-room, and when she went in Richard was sitting there deep in conversation with Cindi.

'Surprise, surprise!' she said. 'I didn't expect to see you!'

He got up, came over and put his arms round her. 'You sounded so fed up on the phone I just had to call in when my session finished,' he said gently. 'I'm sorry I couldn't talk to you right then and there, lovely, but you know how it is!'

She forgot her irritation and disappointment as he smiled down at her. He did care, after all.

'I know. I shouldn't have called you, really, when you were busy!'

Cindi cleared her throat. 'I'm off to bed, so I'll leave you two love-birds to it! Goodnight, Richard.'

'Night, Cindi! And thanks!'

'Have you been here long?' Annabel asked him, when they were sitting on the corner unit with his arm round her shoulders.

'No, only about twenty minutes. Cindi was telling me all about California. It sounds amazing. I really must go there one day!'

She bit her lip. 'I've been at Ben and Jacqui's,' she said abruptly. 'Ben said he thought you'd be off to New York as soon as you got the chance.'

Was it her imagination, or was he avoiding her eyes deliberately?

'I don't know about that,' he said easily. 'I don't want to go until I've made a bit of a name for myself here. I'm working with Lucy Frayn on Saturday, and I'll just have to see what else turns up.'

Annabel looked away, but he caught hold of her shoulders and turned her round to face him.

'Annie, look at me!'

She looked.

'What's on your mind?'

She said nothing. He shook her gently. 'Come on, out with it!'

She laughed, with an effort. 'I was just thinking ... I'll miss you, when you go!'

'You do borrow trouble, don't you?' he said indulgently. 'I'm not going anywhere, am I? Not just now, anyway. Let's worry about all that when it happens, OK?'

She slid her arms round his neck. 'OK.'

As he began to kiss her, she determinedly pushed thoughts of his leaving to the back of her mind. Pretty soon, with his mouth on hers and his hands gentle on her body, the future ceased to matter, and only the present seemed real.

II

Richard was on the telephone to Annabel almost as soon as she walked in to her office the following Monday morning.

'How did the session with Lucy Frayn go?' she asked him.

'It was great. My first time in the national press, Annie! She wants me to do another, maybe two more,' he said, and she couldn't miss the note of triumph in his voice.

'That's fantastic, love! Lucy's not the easiest person in the world to work with, but if she likes you –'

'She seemed to, anyway.'

'I'm glad. You're getting loads of work these days!'

'The more the better,' he said with satisfaction. 'I'm doing a six-day week at the moment, you know!'

'And you talk about me needing a break! Don't overdo it, love, will you?'

'Well, it's not for ever, just till people know my name,' said Richard. 'Besides, I enjoy it. I can't stand sitting around doing nothing, you know that. Actually, Annie, I was going to ask you if you're free tonight?'

Annabel thought rapidly. Her hair needed washing and she had a pile of laundry to do, but Richard was so busy these days she didn't know when she'd get another chance to see him. 'If you can leave it till about eight, that'll give me time to wash my hair and sort myself out a bit,' she said finally.

'OK,' he said, 'do you want to go out to eat or shall I bring some steak and salad and things round?'

'That sounds lovely.'

They sat in Annabel's living-room with the steaks and salad on their knees. Annabel poured two glasses of lager and put a Carole King album on the stereo.

'Mmmm, this steak is delicious, Richard!'

'The butcher near our studio is really good. I believe he supplies some of the top hotels.'

'Our' studio, Annabel thought, he really is coming on.

'Did I tell you I'm going to New York next week?' Richard asked casually.

Annabel stopped eating. 'No. No, you didn't.'

He caught sight of her face. 'Don't look like that, Annie, it's only for a week!'

She relaxed and smiled at him. 'Oh, it's a trip, is it?'

'Yes, it's with *Lady Fair*. You know they have an American edition and a British one? I believe they're doing some kind of exchange thing for their Spring fashion, sending their Fashion Editor, a photographer, and two models over there from England and getting some Americans over here in return.'

'That should be interesting. Oh, Richard ...'

'What is it?'

'It all seems to be happening so fast for you!'

He put his arms round her and held her close. 'I know. I've been very lucky, Annie.'

'No. No, it isn't luck, Richard. You take good pictures and you work hard, and that way you're bound to get noticed! It's just that I – well, we don't seem to see each other as often as we did at first, and I ...'

Was it her imagination or did he look ever-so-slightly impatient with her? Damn, she thought, I always swore I wouldn't try to hang on to him. Why don't I ever learn?

'I see you as often as I can, Annie,' he pointed out gently. 'It won't always be like this, I promise! When I'm a bit better known I'll be able to afford to pick and choose my commissions, but right now I need all the experience I can get!'

At least he seems to think we have some kind of future together, Annabel thought forlornly. She snuggled up to him and smiled repentantly. 'I'm sorry, love. I'm being miserable. I'm just as dedicated to my work as you are to yours, so I really shouldn't grumble!'

'How are things at Annabel Lee?'

'I've seen a couple of really nice new ladies recently. Lisa Smedley has a dreadful old harridan for a mother but she's a very sweet girl and we got her her first job last week, with *Fancy*. Then I saw a lovely girl that Cathy James recommended, and I think we'll probably take her on too.'

'Sounds good. We're both dead lucky, Annie, being able to work at something we enjoy, when you think how many people are bored out of their minds from nine to five every day.'

'Too right! Whenever I see really awful-looking girls who want to be models and ask myself how they can possibly fool themselves they're going to be any good, I remember that. It's worth a try, if your only alternative is some dreary factory!'

She saw Richard off to New York the following week with only a very slight pang. I've just got to be sensible about it, she told herself firmly. I can't expect him to give up his ambitions for me. After all, I wouldn't give up Annabel Lee if he asked me to, and I know he wouldn't dream of asking.

Leonard took her out to dinner twice that week; once to a restaurant and once to Joe and Irene Tilman's home in Golders Green. Annabel didn't really enjoy the latter occasion. The men talked shop for most of the evening and she was left to try and make conversation with the bitter and sarcastic Irene, who had already made it perfectly clear that she disapproved of Annabel anyway.

'Irene Tilman really doesn't like me,' she told Leonard as they drove home.

'Oh, I'm sure she does,' said Leonard loyally. 'You don't want to take too much notice of Irene, Annie. Her bark is much worse than her bite! She talks about Joe as if he were the world's worst, but she's devoted to him, deep down.'

'You could have fooled me,' said Annabel drily. 'She never stopped moaning about him all evening. If that's her idea of devotion, it certainly isn't mine!'

Leonard said no more and she was unreasonably irritated. I wish he'd disagree with me once in a while, she thought.

The day before Richard was due back she received a scribbled, almost indecipherable postcard of Central Park. From what she could gather he was very busy, but enjoying himself enormously.

Richard didn't say very much about his trip to the States, unusually for him, but Annabel, who happened to be extremely busy the week he got back, didn't have the time to wonder why. She gathered that the work had gone well and she admired the two fashion spreads he had done with Lucy Frayn, which appeared in the national daily Lucy worked for the following week.

'They were lovely pictures, Richard!' she said admiringly the next time they met. 'I bet your phone's ringing all the time, isn't it?'

'I have had a few calls,' he admitted. 'To tell you the truth, Annie, I've been asked to do an interview with one of the heavy Sundays.'

'What do you mean, an interview?' asked Annabel, intrigued.

Richard looked slightly embarrassed. 'Apparently they're doing a feature on up-and-coming fashion photographers,' he explained, 'or maybe it's all kinds of photographers, I don't really know. For some reason they seem to have got hold of my name. They want to send a reporter along to talk to me.'

'Richard, that's marvellous! When?'

'Next week, they said. I don't know, though.' He scratched his head and looked rather sheepish. 'I'm not sure I want to do it!'

'But why ever not? It's fantastic publicity!'

'Ye-es, I suppose so. I'm not sure I want to get mixed up in all that trendy Face of the Eighties stuff, though, Annie. It doesn't really sound like my scene. I mean, I'm a working man when you come right down to it. There's no real mystique about what I do!'

'You'll have to tell the reporter that!'

'I just don't know, Annie!'

'I'd be so proud of you!'

'Would you, love?' He smiled, but abstractedly, as if he wasn't really concentrating.

She relaxed in his arms, leaning comfortably against him, studying his strong, square hands, hands that could be so gentle...

'What are you doing for Christmas, Richard?' she asked him, suddenly.

'I don't know. The usual, I suppose. Turkey and plum pudding with the family. How about you?'

'I'll go to Nottingham, to my mother's. There's just the two of us, though, so it's rather quiet.'

'Blimey, you wouldn't know what quietness was in our house at Christmas! It's chaos from start to finish, what with my brother's kids and my sister's baby and my Auntie Joyce and Uncle Tom, and my dad having one too many and sleeping it off in front of the fire – it's always the same!'

'It sounds fun,' said Annabel enviously. 'I can remember having Christmases like that when my dad was alive, but since he died my mother doesn't see so much of his family, and she doesn't have any relatives of her own – or no one close, anyway.'

*

A couple of weeks before Christmas, Annabel's mother rang to confirm their usual holiday arrangements.

'I wondered, Anne,' she said hesitantly over the phone, 'if you would like to ask Leonard to come and spend Christmas with us? He never has done ...'

'All right, Mother, I'll see what he says.'

In fact, she had been thinking of asking Leonard to join them for Christmas ever since she'd known him. The first year, he had told her that he'd decided to return to Canada for the festive season before she could invite him. Last year, she remembered, he had taken up a long-standing invitation to join some old friends in the West Country, so that in fact they had never spent Christmas together. If Richard was going to be involved with his family, Annabel decided, she would ask Leonard to come to Nottingham with her. Why not?

'Nothing would give me more pleasure!' he said formally, taking both her hands in his. 'We'll have a proper celebration, with a Christmas tree and fairy lights.'

'Mother and I don't usually bother, just for the two of us.'

'Well, this year we're going to bother!' he said, slipping an arm round her shoulders.

Annabel normally enjoyed the bustle and goodwill of Christmas but this year it really did seem to be something special. She and Leonard arranged to go to Nottingham on Christmas Eve, and the week prior to that seemed to be one long round of parties.

Christmas at Annabel's mother's home in Nottingham was very enjoyable. Both Mrs Lee and Annabel were caught up in Leonard's enthusiasm for doing everything the traditional way, with holly and paper-chains and home-made mince-pies. Leonard's unobtrusive consideration seemed to break down the barrier of Mrs Lee's reserve, and Annabel marvelled, at tea-time on Christmas Day, when she saw her mother blush like a girl at Leonard's compliments and put on a paper hat from the crackers he had insisted on buying!

There was a carol service her mother wanted to watch on TV. Annabel and Leonard watched, too, at first for lack of anything else to do, but gradually, as the familiar tunes worked their perennial magic, Annabel felt tears sting the back of her eyes. The boy sopranos' voices soared effortlessly, high and clear and true, and Annabel was stirred in a way she had never imagined she could be.

'Lovely, isn't it?' her mother breathed, and she nodded wordlessly. It's beautiful, she thought, it's love and music and Christmas, and I wish Richard were here to share it with me. Later, when Leonard and her mother were absorbed in the early-evening movie, she tiptoed out into the hall, intending to telephone Richard and wish him a Happy Christmas. She got his home number from Directory Enquiries and dialled, her fingers trembling.

'Hello?' came a raucous voice at the other end. It sounded as if the Reddings' family Christmas was every bit as riotous as Richard had said it would be. She could hear shrieks and squeals in the background.

'Could I speak to Richard, please?' she murmured.

'You'll have to speak up, dear! Can't hear you!'

She looked anxiously at the door of the living-room. 'Richard?'

'Righto, I'll fetch him.'

The receiver clattered down and it seemed an age before she heard his voice.

'It's me. Annie!'

'Oh, hello!' He sounded surprised.

'I won't keep you, love, I just wanted to wish you a happy Christmas!'

'To you, too!' he said.

'I hope you don't mind me ringing.'

'No, 'course I don't, it's nice to hear from you. Are you having a good time, love?'

She nodded, and then, realizing he couldn't see her, said, 'Yes, I am.'

'Good. It's like a madhouse here! I'll see you soon, OK?'

She swallowed the lump that seemed to have appeared in her throat. 'OK. 'Bye, love.'

As it turned out, Annabel had to stay up in Nottingham until after the New Year, as her mother developed a heavy cold and Annabel didn't like to leave her alone. Suzy and Gillian held the fort at 'Annabel Lee' and Richard came round to the flat the second evening after she had returned to London. He carried a wicker basket, and she frowned as she let him in.

'What have you got there?'

'I promised you a special present, remember?' he said, putting the basket down and holding her close for a moment. 'Don't you want to open it?'

She did so. At the bottom of the basket a tiny ball of black and white fluff was sleeping. It opened its eyes and let out a plaintive mew.

'A kitten! Oh, Richard, it's adorable!'

He grinned. 'I thought you'd like it ... or rather her.'

Annabel cradled the tiny animal in her cupped hands. It put out its tiny pink tongue and licked her fingers. She stroked its soft fur, crooning.

'Who's a pretty baby, then? Who's a pretty pussy-cat?'

The kitten wriggled out of her hands and set about exploring its new home on tentative black paws, its absurd pointed tail sticking straight up in the air. Annabel hugged Richard gratefully.

'She's wonderful, darling. The nicest present I've ever had!'

'I thought she'd be company for you,' he said quietly.

It didn't register at first. Then she turned to him, puzzled. 'What do you mean, company?'

'Well ...' He hesitated. 'Look, Annie, I think I'd better tell you right away.'

'Tell me? Tell me what?'

'I'm going to New York.'

'Another trip?' she said, knowing already that it wasn't.

'No, not a trip. I've had a letter from Dean Schuster ... you've heard of him?'

'Who hasn't?'

Dean Schuster, photographer and film-maker extraordinary, of course Annabel had heard of him.

'I went to see him with some of my stuff when I was over there on the *Lady Fair* trip. He seemed to like it, and he said he'd let me know if there was anything he could do for me. This letter came just after the New Year; he wants me over there right away.'

'Right away,' Annabel echoed.

'Well ... I'm going next week.'

'Next week.' She raised stricken eyes to his. In two strides he was across the room, crushing her in his arms.

'I know, Annie, I know. I wish –'

'What?'

'I wish there was some other way.'

She pulled away, refusing to meet his eyes. 'Well, there isn't. I suppose I've always known you'd go, sooner or later; it's just come a bit sooner than I expected, that's all.'

'Don't be like that. Don't be bitter.'

Don't be bitter. Someone else had said that to her once, a lifetime ago. Who was it ... ah, yes, Jacqui. Jacqui with her nice safe loving husband, Jacqui with all her security, Jacqui who could not possibly know what it was like to love someone and have your heart torn apart by his careless kindness, what it was like to be loved and then left and forgotten ...

'I'm not bitter.' She forced a bright smile. 'It's a wonderful opportunity for you. Of course you must go.' She could not look at him.

'It's hard for me, too, Annie.'

'Why? It's what you want. It's what you've always wanted!'

'I'll miss you,' he said simply.

She looked up, and their eyes met, and suddenly she was in his arms and he was kissing her with a frantic, desperate urgency, and she was crying and almost, almost begging him not to go ... but not quite.

'How long have we got?' she asked, calm again.

'I fly out on Wednesday.'

She calculated. Wednesday. Eight days away. So little time, so little time left. Wednesday.

12

'I don't get it!' Cindi shook her dark head and looked blankly at Annabel.

'What do you mean?'

Cindi spoke slowly, as if she were addressing a small child. 'Well, why in Heaven's name don't you go to New York with him?'

It was Annabel's turn to look blank. 'He hasn't asked me to!'

Cindi sighed. 'Honestly, you two just kill me. You're so proud, both of you. OK, he hasn't asked you, but couldn't that be because he figures you'll say no? You've been doing this independent career-girl bit ever since he met you, so how is he to know you want to go to New York with him? I tell you, Annie, much as I love flying, I'd quit tomorrow if I met a guy who meant half as much to me as Richard means to you!'

Annabel managed a rueful smile. 'Oh, Cindi! And I thought you were liberated!'

'Liberated? What does that mean? The only kind of liberation that makes any sense is for people to do the things they want to do, the things that will make them happy.'

'Maybe you're right.'

'Sure I'm right.' Cindi patted Annabel's hand. 'I don't know much about business, Annie, but wouldn't it be possible for Suzy to take over Annabel Lee? Buy out your share, something like that?'

Annabel thought rapidly. Suzy and young Gillian were

just about as capable of running 'Annabel Lee' as she was. Maybe it was possible. Maybe she wouldn't have to say good- bye to Richard on Wednesday, after all, or only for the little time it would take to arrange things here. She could fly out in a couple of weeks, join him in New York. Cindi was right, she had been too proud to show him how much she cared that he was leaving.

It was only when she got into the office the following day that she realized how impossible it was. To leave all this ... she looked around, at the decor she had chosen so lovingly, at the models she had turned from shy beginners into confident professionals, at the complete, comfortable world she had built up for herself. And there was Leonard. How could she ever leave Leonard, after all he had done for her? Living with Richard in New York would mean no job and no money, or not unless she went back to modelling again. Keeping house in a tiny apartment somewhere, hang- ing around waiting for Richard to come home from a day's shooting, being an anonymous photographer's lady instead of Annabel Lee, well-known agent. She couldn't do it, not even for Richard, not even if it broke her heart.

And then it was Tuesday, and he was leaving, and he had come round to her flat to say goodbye. They sat in the living-room, hand in hand, listening to a James Taylor album. It was the record that Annabel had played the first time they had spent the night together and she knew she would never be able to play it again without thinking of him.

'Annie?'

'Yes?'

'It may not be for ever, you know. I'll be back ...'

She shook her head. 'You mustn't make any promises, Richard. It's a fantastic chance for you and you can't tell what might happen.'

'Would you like me to write to you?'

'I don't see the point. It's best to make a clean break, don't you think? No sense in prolonging it. It's better this way!' Her lips felt stiff and cold.

'If you say so.'

Already, almost imperceptibly, they had moved away from each other, as if to emphasize the miles that would soon be between them. Oh, Richard, she thought, I can't bear it, we were so close, I can't bear this coldness!

Suddenly he took her hand. 'Annie!'

Panic gripped her. Don't ask me, she thought desperately, don't ask me to go with you, I don't know what I might say. 'Cheer up!' she said flippantly. 'You'll have a great time over there and forget you ever knew me, I expect. Anyway, it's been nice knowing you, and we've had a good run for our money!'

'Don't, Annie!'

'What?'

'Don't try to sound so ... hard. It isn't like you!'

'You think I ... I want to ...'

Her voice broke. With one finger, he wiped away the tears she had hardly known were there.

'I'm making it worse. I'd better go.'

She nodded, not trusting herself to speak, and walked with him to the front door. He turned and took both her hands in his.

'Darling, I was never any good with words, but I want you to know that ... I do care,' he said hoarsely. 'It's the hardest thing I've ever done, leaving you. It breaks me up to see you cry.'

'I'm not crying,' said Annabel, lifting her chin up proudly.

'That's my girl. Well ... thank you for everything.'

'Goodbye, Richard,' she whispered.

The door closed behind him. He had gone. She heard his footsteps go down the front path and felt as if she would choke on the pain in her throat. She heard the front gate click. His footsteps were fainter now as he walked away. She stood in the hallway, quite silently, until she couldn't hear them any more. Then she walked slowly back into the living room and turned the record over, for something to do. James Taylor sang. Music to say goodbye to.

Annabel cried.

How do you forget someone? she asked herself savagely through the next few awful, painful weeks. When everywhere you go you've been with him, when everything you do is dull and flat because he's not there to do it with you, when all your songs remind you of him, when people you both know mention him, so casually, and your heart turns over at the sound of his name. How are you supposed to forget?

It couldn't have worked out, anyway, she told herself. We're too alike: too ambitious, too selfish, too dedicated. I was right when I told him we'd had a good run for our money. I knew it couldn't last, I always knew he'd go, one day. We had all that time, we were happy together, and that's more than I ever expected. I've been lucky. I've made my choice. I chose Annabel Lee, and Leonard, and it's no use wishing that things had worked out differently.

All the sensible, comforting illusions – but still there were times when she woke at night with tears drying on her cheeks, and lay wide-eyed and sleepless, staring into the darkness, wondering where he was, what he was doing, if he was thinking of her and wondering whether his decision had been the right one ...

She still had Leonard. Kind, comforting, unobtrusive Leonard, who never asked her why she'd grown so thin and pale, but showed his concern for her with his usual thoughtfulness and consideration. I wonder if he suspects, Annabel thought, once, when she turned round and surprised him looking at her with such an odd mixture of affection, tenderness and regret. Still, it's all over now; no need to feel I owe him any explanations any more.

Work took up a great deal of Annabel's time over the next few weeks. With most of the monthly magazines already planning their summer fashions, it meant several trips abroad for the Annabel Lee models, with all the organizational problems that trips brought with them. At times, when she was joking with Suzy in the office, or admiring a particularly nice set of pictures of one of the Annabel Lee girls, Annabel -could almost forget there had ever been such a person as Richard Redding. She was reminded of him, sickeningly, a few weeks later when Ben Lawrence came back from a lightning visit to New York and popped into the office to see her.

'Ben! When did you get back?' cried Annabel, giving him a hug.

'This morning,' he said, yawning. 'I'm still a bit jet-lagged, actually, but I thought I'd call in on my way home.'

Suzy brought him a cup of coffee.

'Did you have a good time?'

'Pretty good, yes.'

Quite casually, Suzy asked the question that Annabel wouldn't have dreamed of asking.

'Did you see anything of what's-his-name, the guy you used to work with? The good-looking one – Richard?'

'I called him, but he was out of town on a session,' said Ben easily.

Neither of them seemed to notice Annabel, standing rooted to the spot, her heart thumping and her mouth suddenly dry. Suppose Ben had seen him? Suppose he had sent some message?

Ben took a copy of American *Vogue* out of his canvas hold-all. 'I got this, though. Richard did the cover, and some of the stuff inside. He's doing fantastically well over there, I hear. Everyone is talking about him. He's been featured in goodness knows how many glossies and even a talk show on TV. A proper little trendy!'

He must hate it, Annabel thought. He never wanted that. Still, how should I know what he wants? He could have changed ...

'These are lovely!' said Suzy, flicking through the magazine. 'He *has* done well, hasn't he? Look Annie, they're beautiful!'

'Beautiful,' Annabel echoed, looking at Richard's photographs without really seeing them.

'Aren't you jealous, Ben?' Gillian asked.

'Who, me? No chance!' said Ben with a grin. 'I wouldn't live in New York if you paid me. It's all too fast and frantic for me. If I had to work in the States it would be in San Francisco, but I'm perfectly happy in London really!'

'Who's the model?' asked Suzy, who was still idly looking through the American magazine. 'She's a lovely girl!'

'The model? Oh, yes, it's that ... er ... what's-her-name. Biggest thing in the States at the moment,' said Ben vaguely. 'She's done a couple of movies, too, I believe. Leonora something. Actually, if you want a bit of gossip, girls, I did hear that she and young Richard were pretty friendly. More than friendly, in fact!'

The photographs blurred in front of Annabel's eyes. She clenched her teeth so hard that her jaw ached.

'Are you all right, Annie?' Suzy asked.

'Mmm. Something in my eye! I'd better just pop out to the loo!'

She locked herself in the Ladies and splashed water on her face before leaning hopelessly against the mirror, feeling the glass cool and hard against her flushed cheeks. Leonora. Leonora something. The biggest thing in the States. I hate her. I hate him, too, for making me love him. And I thought it was all over. I thought I'd forgotten ...

That night, after work, she drove straight to Leonard's flat.

'I need a drink,' she said, striding in. Leonard poured her a Martini and handed it to her silently.

'Had a bad day?' he asked, concerned.

She nodded, and began to pace the floor, stiff with tension.

'Poor Annie. You're all wound up,' he said affectionately.

'Just sit down and relax and tell me about it!'

'There's nothing to tell. It's just that things have been getting on top of me.'

He sat down in an armchair and held out his arms to her. 'Come here, baby. I'll make it better!'

He held her while she sobbed, patting her shoulders, pushing her tear-wet hair back from her hot face, and finally producing another clean white handkerchief and commanding her to blow her nose.

'There,' he said tenderly. 'Better?'

She managed a watery smile. 'Oh, Leonard, you're so good to me!'

He smiled, and put his arms round her. She rested her head against his cashmere sweater, feeling curiously peaceful and drained of all feeling. Perhaps this was the way love should be, after all, this undemanding affection, gentle and comforting, and not violent emotions and uncertainty. She sniffed and blew her nose again.

'I must look a sight!' she said, taking her little make-up mirror out of her handbag and shuddering at her blotchy, tear-stained reflection.

'You always look beautiful to me, Annie!' Leonard said. It was the kind of remark he had often made before, the kind of remark that had always made her feel faintly uneasy, but this time she just felt warm and loved and reassured. She smiled at him, and began to repair her make-up.

'Annie?'

'Mmmm?' she said, busy with her powder-compact.

'Annie – will you – that is ... would you consider marrying me?'

Slowly, she put the compact down, and turned to face him, incredulous. 'But I ... but, Leonard ...'

He laughed nervously. 'Don't look so staggered, Annie! The idea must have entered your head before, surely? We're both free and over twenty-one; we've known each other for

124

nearly four years, and you've always known I was in love with you!'

'Oh, Leonard!' she said helplessly.

'I'm sure we could be happy,' he said, stammering slightly and suddenly seeming much younger. 'We get on well – you've always said that. I wouldn't want you to give up the agency, not till we had a family, and not even then if you didn't want to. I do love you so very much, and I want to have the right to take care of you for always. If you'll allow me to, that is. Please, Annie, please say you will!'

'Leonard –'

'Do you love me?' he demanded, seizing her hands.

'Well – well, yes – I ...'

'Don't say it if you don't mean it, or if you're not sure. I've got love enough for both of us and in time you'll love me, I know you will!'

'I don't need time,' she said calmly. 'I love you now. I've always loved you, but I didn't realize it. I thought that love was ... something else; but this is love, after all, isn't it? Getting on well, and taking care of each other, like you said. We'll be happy, Leonard!'

'Then you will? You'll marry me?'

'Yes.'

He jumped up, as excited as a schoolboy. 'This calls for a celebration! I'll open some champagne! Mrs Elliott! Mrs Elliott!'

Annabel laughed. 'Oh, Leonard!'

'You don't know how long I've waited or how much I've hoped this day would come! Oh, Annie, you'll never regret it, I promise!'

For a moment, she laid her cheek against his hair. 'No, love. No, I won't regret it.'

13

'You called me, Mr Leonard?'

Mrs Elliott appeared at the door, wiping her floury hands on her apron.

'Yes. Could you bring a bottle of champagne and two, no, three glasses, please? We're celebrating!'

Mrs Elliott raised her eyebrows in polite enquiry.

'Annabel and I are getting married!'

Mrs Elliott flushed, and looked taken aback. 'Really! Oh, well, in that case I'd like to wish you both every happiness!'

I wonder if she means that, Annabel thought. I know she's never thought much of me! I wonder if she'll want to stay on after we're married? After we're married ... it doesn't seem real, somehow!

Leonard put his arm round her. 'Thank you very much! Now, how about that champagne?'

Mrs Elliott disappeared as silently as she had come and Leonard beamed at Annabel. 'We'd better ring your mother, darling. Start making plans!'

Annabel spread her hands helplessly, laughing at his enthusiasm. 'Hold your horses, love. We've only been engaged for about three minutes. I haven't had time to think! I know mother will be delighted – in fact she's probably been expecting it – but maybe we should think it out a bit before we call her!'

Mrs Elliott reappeared with a bottle of chilled champagne and three glasses. Leonard opened it deftly and they drank. 'To Mrs Leonard Francis,' Leonard said, raising his glass.

Annabel laughed, and even Mrs Elliott smiled as she sipped her champagne.

'We'll have to move from here,' Leonard said suddenly, looking around at the old-fashioned furniture in his living-room. For the first time, Annabel realized that getting married would mean leaving the cosy flat and Cindi, and she felt a pang of homesickness. I'm being ridiculous, she told herself.

'We'll have to look round a few estate agents on Saturday and see what's available,' he decided. 'I wouldn't mind staying in this area somewhere, though.'

'Oh, yes, anywhere round here,' Annabel agreed. 'It's handy for work and most of my friends aren't far away.'

She was beginning to feel quite excited and some of the unreality was wearing off. I'm getting married, she thought. Me, Annabel Lee. I'm going to be a bride. I'm going to be Mrs Leonard Francis!

'Let's ring mother now!' she said eagerly.

'Do you want to tell her, or shall I?'

Annabel thought for a moment. 'You tell her, or ask her for my hand, or whatever you have to do!'

Leonard dialled the Nottingham number. Annabel's mother answered the phone almost immediately.

'Margaret? It's Leonard! No ... no, nothing's wrong, far from it. Annabel and I have some good news for you. We're going to get married! Yes ... yes ... that's if you have no objection, of course.'

After a few moments he handed the receiver to Annabel. 'Your mother wants a word with the bride!'

'Hello? Mother?' said Annabel.

Her mother sounded close to tears, the most emotional that Annabel could ever remember her being. 'Oh, Anne!' she said in a choked voice. 'I can't tell you how pleased I am for you. Leonard's a good man, a kind man; he'll take care of you.'

'I know, mother. I'm –'

'Are you happy, Anne? Are you sure?'

'Yes, mother. Quite sure!'

When she had put the phone down, Annabel said, 'Mother did seem pleased, love. I think she thought I was going to end up an old maid!'

Leonard laughed fondly. 'Some chance of that! I've been so worried over the last few years that someone else would steal you away from under my nose. All those handsome young fellows you work with.' Annabel's smile faded, and she remembered Ben, and the cover-girl from America, and Richard. It seemed much longer ago than just that morning that she had heard about Leonora.

'What's the matter, Annie?'

She gave herself a little mental shake. 'Nothing. I was just thinking ... let's drive up to Jacqui and Ben's and tell them the good news!'

'Good idea. I've probably got another bottle of bubbly in the fridge we can take up there.'

They drove over to Hampstead in Leonard's car, and rang the Lawrences' doorbell. Marie-Claude opened the door. 'Monsieur he is in bed, Madame watches the television,' she informed them. Leonard and Annabel went into the living-room to find Jacqui curled up on the sofa watching a play. She jumped up when they came in.

'Annie! Leonard! What a nice surprise!'

'We're interrupting you,' said Annabel gently.

'What ... oh, not at all. It's a silly piece. I was just being lazy tonight. Ben's whacked out with jet-lag so he's gone to bed. Can I get you a drink?'

Annabel felt suddenly shy. 'We've brought some champagne, actually,' she said.

'Champagne?'

'We're celebrating!' said Leonard, unable to contain himself any longer. 'Annie and I are getting married!'

'Married? Oh, Annie, how lovely! I don't believe it!'

Annabel nodded. 'It's true!'

Jacqui hugged her warmly, seeming near to tears herself. 'Oh, love, I'm so happy for you. Truly I am!' She beamed at them both. 'It couldn't happen to two nicer people! I'm going to fetch Ben, and then we'll open that bottle of champagne!'

'Don't wake him, Jacqui,' Annabel protested. 'He must be done in!'

'Oh, nonsense. This is a special occasion. Won't be a minute!'

A few moments later Ben came into the room, yawning, wearing a tatty pair of pyjama trousers and one slipper. Annabel hugged him. 'Ben, love, she shouldn't have woken you!'

'Rubbish! I've been asleep hours, and anyway I don't want to miss this, do I now?' he said. He kissed Annabel and shook Leonard warmly by the hand. 'All the very, very best to both of you!'

All Annabel's friends and colleagues seemed to react the same way when she telephoned them from the office the next morning. Suzy, whose efficient manner hid the most sentimental of hearts, burst into tears as soon as Annabel told her and insisted on sending Gillian out for celebration cream buns!

'What are you crying for, you soft thing?' said Annabel, not far from tears herself. She was touched to the heart by her friends' kindness and encouragement, by how very much they all seemed to care.

'It's ... all so romantic,' wept Suzy. Annabel fetched her a tissue and helped her to mop her streaming eyes.

'What did Cindi say when you told her?' Suzy asked curiously. 'She doesn't believe in marriage, does she?'

Annabel laughed. 'Oh, Cindi's more of a romantic than you'd think, deep down,' she said. 'She's a bit cynical about marriage, it's true, but then so would I be if my father was on his fourth and my mother her second! She's doing a run to Dallas this week, though, so I shan't see her till Thursday.'

In fact, Annabel found the prospect of telling Cindi about her engagement a little bit embarrassing. It wasn't just that Cindi had often said she didn't believe in marriage, nor even having to tell her she was moving out of the flat that made her feel awkward. It was just that Cindi was the only one of her friends who had known for certain about Richard. However much she tried to hide the truth from herself, in the end she was forced to admit that she wasn't absolutely sure what Cindi's reaction would be.

'Jeez! I've had enough!' Cindi cried, coming into the flat on Thursday evening and dumping her bags in the middle of the living-room floor. She peeled off her smart navy jacket, unfastened the scarf at her throat and kicked off her shoes.

'Want a coffee? It's just perked!' Annabel told her.

Cindi ran her hands through her shiny dark hair. 'That sounds wonderful!' she said, collapsing into a sag-bag.

Annabel brought coffee for Cindi and herself.

'How's things?' her friend asked, stretching her long legs and sipping her coffee gratefully. 'Aaaah! That's better!'

'I have some news for you,' said Annabel carefully.

Cindi raised her eyebrows. 'Yeah? Good or bad?'

'Good.'

'Well?'

'I'm getting married in June.'

Cindi stared, speechless, and put down her coffee cup. 'You're getting married?' she repeated.

'Yes. To Leonard,' said Annabel hastily. 'He asked me on Tuesday, and we don't think there's any point in waiting any longer than we have to. You must arrange to be here, Cindi. You'll have to swap schedules with someone.'

As Cindi still didn't say anything, Annabel's voice trailed off into silence. 'Well? Don't just sit there,' she joked, awkwardly. 'Say something!'

For answer, Cindi got up, came over to Annabel and took both her hands in hers, looking intently into her eyes. 'Are you sure it's what you want, Annie?'

Annabel looked back at her steadily. 'Yes. Yes, I'm sure, or I would never have said yes.'

Cindi sighed, and leaned back. Slowly, she nodded. 'Maybe you're right. Security, safety, maybe those are the right reasons to marry. I mean, how would I know?'

'It's not just that!' cried Annabel, stung. 'I love Leonard, Cindi. I always have! He's so good to me. I'm terribly fond of him!'

Cindi still looked thoughtful. 'I know, love. I know you are, but what about Richard?'

Annabel looked blank, and her mouth went hard. 'What about Richard? He's gone, it's over and he's gone, and I'm marrying Leonard. There's no more to be said!'

Cindi nodded again, and then suddenly she smiled. 'OK, Annie, I hope you'll be happy! Leonard's a good guy, though I'm not sure I'll forgive him for stealing the best room-mate I ever had in my life!'

Gradually, as time went on, the feeling of unreality that had troubled Annabel at the beginning of her engagement wore off. It's hard to get used to knowing what the future has in store, she thought. I suppose that's what they mean by security. I'm going to marry Leonard. He's always going to be there, loving me, looking after me, and I'll never be on my own again. She sat at her desk in the office, twisting her ring round and round on her engagement finger, and smiling to herself with a kind of quiet contentment. It's like coming home after a long holiday, she thought. I must be doing the right thing.

Leonard came round to the flat one evening to go through some estate agents' lists, and before he left, he said, 'Oh, by the way, Annie, I've got to go to Edinburgh again on Tuesday. Do you want to come?'

Annabel shook her head. 'I can't really, love. We've got a couple of trips going off next week and I ought to be here. Will you be away long?'

'I should be back on Friday. Maybe Thursday night if I'm lucky.'

He phoned Annabel from Edinburgh on Thursday lunchtime. 'I'm coming home, darling!' he said exuberantly. 'I'm all finished here, so I'm setting off now. I'll be with you tomorrow!'

'Lovely. I'll buy some steaks, shall I?'

'Mmmm. And keep yourself looking beautiful for me. I've missed you, darling.'

'I've missed you, too,' said Annabel, smiling.

Britt Sonderstrøm, one of the agency's most popular models, was in the office on Friday morning, making Annabel, Suzy and Gillian laugh with her imitation of a client she hadn't got on with. The telephone rang and Gillian answered it.

'Phoebe Elliott for you, Annie!'

Annabel wrinkled her brow. 'Doesn't ring a bell. Could you find out who she is and what she wants, Gillian?'

'She says she's Leonard's housekeeper,' said Gillian after a moment.

'Oh, Lord,' said Annabel in mock dismay. 'I never realized ... fancy her being called Phoebe!'

Suzy giggled.

'OK, Gillian, put her through!'

At first she didn't recognize Mrs Elliott's voice. She frowned in puzzlement. 'Mrs Elliott? Is that you?'

The sound at the end of the line was like a muffled sob.

'Mrs Elliott?'

'Oh, Miss ... Annabel, I don't know how to tell you!'

Icy fingers of fear clutched Annabel's heart. She gripped the receiver. 'Just tell me,' she said, in a voice she hardly recognized.

'It's Mr Leonard. There's been an accident. A lorry on the A1 ... it was a multiple pile-up.'

'And Leonard?' Annabel whispered.

'He was killed instantly.'

14

Annabel put the telephone down. Over at the other side of the room Suzy and Britt were still chuckling, and Gillian stood in the doorway smiling at them both. Outside, in the mews, a car started up and roared away. She heard somebody whistling and, in the distance, the sound of a train. She sat, silently, waiting to feel something; grief, despair, anything apart from this huge disbelief.

'Annie?'

It was Suzy. 'Annie, are you all right? What's happened?'

'Leonard's dead,' said Annabel tonelessly.

It was like a film, she decided, a movie slowed down so that the actors were frozen in one position. Gillian, immobile in the doorway, her hand to her mouth. Suzy, leaning back in her chair, staring at Annabel in horror. Britt broke the silence, saying something in Swedish.

'But what ... how ...' Suzy began.

'A car crash on the A1. A lorry jack-knifed at a roundabout. It wasn't his fault, but then it wouldn't be. Leonard's a terribly careful driver, you know. He used to worry about me in my car and complain if I drove too fast. It couldn't have been his fault.'

'Oh, love. Oh, Annie,' said Suzy brokenly.

Gillian suddenly came to life. 'I'll make some tea,' she said hastily. 'Hot, sweet tea, for shock. That's the best thing, isn't it?'

But I don't take sugar, Annabel thought irrelevantly; sweet tea will probably make me sick. Shock? Is that what I feel?

Suzy came over and put her arms round her. 'What are

you going to do, Annie? Do you have to go round to Leonard's place, or what? What did his housekeeper say?'

Annabel tried to think. 'She said that ... the firm was taking care of all the arrangements. The arrangements. That means the funeral, doesn't it? I don't think I'd be any good at arranging a funeral!'

'Don't, Annie!'

'Leonard would. He always knew what to do. I went to him every time I had a problem, and he always saw the way out for me. Now I don't even know how to arrange his funeral!'

Suzy gripped her hand tightly. Gillian came in with a mug of strong, milky tea. She gave it to Annabel but her hands were shaking so much that she could hardly lift it to her lips, and Suzy had to hold it for her. She swallowed a mouthful, grimacing. 'Ugh! It's horrible!'

'Try to drink some, Annie!' Gillian advised.

Annabel choked down a couple more mouthfuls. Suzy and Gillian looked at each other helplessly.

'I want to go home,' she said.

'To your flat? Is Cindi there?'

'No, she's on a flight. I want to go home,' Annabel repeated.

'Love, I don't think you should be alone,' said Suzy gently.

'I want to go home.'

'Gillian,' said Suzy, 'is Jacqui Lawrence working today?'

'I'll just check. Hang on ... no, she isn't.'

'Well, can you call her, please? Explain what's happened. Tell her I'm taking Annie home and ask her if she can be there right away.'

Almost as soon as they reached the flat, the doorbell rang. It was Jacqui, her fair hair dishevelled, her beautiful face pale with concern.

'I came as soon as I could, Suzy,' she said breathlessly. 'Unfortunately it's Marie-Claude's day off so I had to dump the kids on my mother. I can't believe it's really true. How is Annie?'

Suzy shook her head. 'Very strange. I think she's in shock, Jacqui. She hasn't cried or anything. She just sits there without saying anything, or chatters about what a good driver Leonard is ... was.'

'It would be better if she could cry.'

'I know. Maybe you could get through to her.'

Jacqui went with Suzy into the living-room, where Annabel sat quite still, looking across the room at nothing.

'Honey, I don't know how to say how sorry I am,' Jacqui began, tears stinging the back of her eyes. 'I don't suppose anything I can say will be any comfort, but if there's anything, anything at all that Ben and I can do to help, you only have to say.'

Annabel almost smiled. 'I know. You're very good, both of you.'

Jacqui sat down beside her.

'I must go,' said Suzy. 'Listen, do you think I should phone round and tell people? I don't suppose Annie will feel like doing it.'

'Yes, I think you should,' said Jacqui worriedly. 'Give Ben a call and tell him I'm here, Suzy.'

'Thank you,' said Annabel suddenly.

Suzy left, and Jacqui and Annabel sat together in silence.

'What about your mother, Annie?' Jacqui asked gently at last.

'I should tell her, shouldn't I? I'm not sure I can, though. If I don't tell people it seems less real, somehow.'

'She'll come down, won't she, when she knows?'

'I suppose so. We'll have to make a bed up for her in here. Jacqui, I can't. I can't tell her. Would you mind ...'

'I'll do it,' said Jacqui, glad to have something to do.

There were no tears. There was nothing but a hard dry ache in Annabel's heart that made her feel as if she were looking at the world through glass. Her mother arrived, wept, and was comforted. Annabel sat up half the night with her, holding her hands, bringing her endless cups of tea and cigarettes, listening to her sob and say what a wonderful person Leonard had been, and agreeing without really feeling anything. Cindi came back from her flight and was appalled at the news, and even more at Annabel's apparent acceptance of it.

'She's got to crack, Jacqui,' she said worriedly, when Annabel showed no signs of real mourning. 'It's unnatural, and terribly bad for her!'

'I know, but what can we do?' Jacqui replied.

Cindi, more and more alarmed by Annabel's emotional state, dragged her off to the doctor the day before Leonard's funeral. He prescribed Valium. On the morning of the funeral, Cindi stood over Annabel while she swallowed two pills, and then took the bottle away.

'Why? I'm not going to take an overdose!' said Annabel.

'All the same, I'll keep these,' said Cindi grimly.

All through the nightmare of Leonard's funeral service, Annabel's feeling of total unreality persisted. She stood between Ben and her mother, in a borrowed black coat, listening to the minister's comforting platitudes and wondering what she, Annabel Lee, could possibly be doing there. She heard her mother's muffled sobs; saw Jacqui with tears running down her face; Suzy with Gillian's arm round her; Mrs Elliott, pale and composed. After it was over, she received everyone's condolences, dry-eyed.

The flowers were beautiful, Annabel thought irrelevantly, crosses and wreaths and sprays and big bouquets. It was spring, and daffodils were dancing in the churchyard, and the sky was the newly-washed April blue, and she knew at last that she was never going to see Leonard again. She would never love him, never rest her tired head on his shoulder and let him soothe her troubles away, never give him the little red-curled daughter he longed for ...

And still she could not cry.

She saw her mother off on the train to Nottingham. She thanked Jacqui and Ben for everything they had done and insisted that they go home and leave her now that the funeral was over. Ever since Suzy had told them one or other of them had been with her; Jacqui had hardly left her side, and the strain was beginning to tell on her. All the same, she managed to have a quiet word with Cindi before she and Ben went home.

'Don't worry,' Cindi said. 'I won't leave her. I have a couple days' leave due; I'll take them right now.'

'I'm terribly worried about her still,' Jacqui admitted.

Neither Cindi nor Annabel felt much like eating, but in the end Cindi prepared omelettes and they sat on the living-room floor to eat them.

'It seems so awful,' Annabel said. 'Last week, everything was fine. I was getting married in a couple of months, and then ... one jack-knifing lorry and it's all over! Leonard might just as well not have existed. Last week he was alive, and now he's dead!'

'But he did exist,' said Cindi gently, thinking that encouraging Annabel to talk and explore her feelings might possibly unlock her grief. 'He existed, and he loved you, and he made your life pretty good and pretty happy and that was what it was all for!'

'I don't think it was *for* anything,' said Annabel bleakly. 'Oh, Cindi, it all seems so pointless, so futile.'

'I know. I don't have any religious faith, Annie, so I can't promise you'll be together again one day, but you *were* happy, and that's worth something in this crazy world!'

Just then there was a scratching at the door and Cleo, Annabel's half-grown kitten, padded into the room. Annabel picked her up, smoothing the soft fur. Cleo purred and settled down on her lap.

'I know why I can't cry,' Annabel burst out suddenly.

'Why?'

'Because I feel guilty!'

She began to stroke Cleo's fur compulsively, and the little cat wriggled in protest.

'Why guilty?'

'Oh, Cindi, because of Richard! All that time I was seeing Richard, loving him, sleeping with him even, and never thinking about what I might be doing to Leonard.'

'But Leonard didn't know.'

Now Annabel had started to talk about it, she didn't seem able to stop. 'I'm not sure of that, even. How could he not know, or not suspect? And he never said anything, never did anything, never stopped loving me, just waited to pick up the pieces when it all went wrong! Do you know what he said when he asked me to marry him, Cindi? He said it didn't matter if I didn't love him, because he had love enough for both of us! I didn't deserve him, Cindi. I didn't deserve that kind of man, or that kind of love. I've never loved anyone that unselfishly. I don't think I'm capable of it!' She was trembling.

'Who knows what sort of love each one of us deserves? Life doesn't work like that!' Cindi murmured.

'But I must have hurt him. I used him, Cindi. Every time things went wrong for me, at work, or with Richard, I'd go flying over to Leonard's place and let him take over for me. I made myself out to be so independent, but really I couldn't stand on my own at all. I needed Leonard. I needed him, and I used him, and I hurt him, and now he's dead and it's all my fault!'

Cindi took Annabel's shaking hands in hers. 'Now listen, Annie,' she said. 'You mustn't be too hard on yourself and you certainly mustn't blame yourself for what happened. I don't believe Leonard knew you were seeing anyone else, but even if he did, didn't it ever occur to you that he might just be content to wait until it blew over? As for leaning on him, using him, well, didn't he want it that way? Didn't he encourage you to share your troubles with him? All he wanted was to take care of you and make you happy, and since you've been engaged he's been like a new man! You made him happy, Annabel. You were all he ever wanted and he died a happy man. How many people can say that?'

At last, the tears came. Cindi was there, holding her, rocking her like a child until she fell at last into an exhausted sleep. Then she wriggled out of Annabel's clinging arms and laid her gently on the floor, finding a cushion for her head and covering her with a blanket. She tiptoed out of the room and telephoned Jacqui.

'Jacqui? Listen, I've just tucked Annie up. She's been crying her heart out.'

'Thank God for that. It's just what she needed.'

'Yes. I think she was hung up because she felt guilty.'

There was a pause.

'Guilty about Richard Redding, you mean?'

'I didn't know you knew! Annie told me no one did!'

'I can put two and two together, Cindi. I knew from the start there was going to be something between those two – I could feel it. I've known Annabel for years, don't forget. I probably shouldn't say this, but it worried me that she might be marrying Leonard on the rebound.'

'Me, too, but she swore it was more than that, and Annie's usually pretty honest!'

'With us, yes, but is she always honest with herself?'

'How many of us are? Still, she's had a good weep, and now she's sleeping. I think that's the worst over.'

Annabel returned to the office the following week, pale and quiet but apparently fit for work again. She was still taking tranquillizers, which worried Suzy and Gillian, but she seemed to be oddly comforted by the familiar rhythm of office routine. At first, everyone was a little embarrassed, both models and clients, deliberately avoiding mentioning Leonard, or weddings, or anything that might possibly upset Annabel.

'Please don't mind me,' she said awkwardly, when one of the girls stopped half-way through discussing a friend's wedding plans.

'But it seems so tactless ... I am sorry, Annie!' the girl said, biting her lip.

'Look, I don't want to be treated like Dresden china,' said

Annabel, with something of her old spirit. 'I notice how everyone is avoiding mentioning Leonard's name, and we can't go on like that.'

'I don't think any of us know how to cope with death today,' said Suzy gently.

A couple of weeks after the funeral, Annabel went to see Leonard's lawyer, who told her that apart from a legacy to Mrs Elliott, Leonard had left her all his money.

Knowing that 'Annabel Lee' was safe was consoling, of course, but in some strange way Annabel was more depressed than when she first went back to work. Knowing how much Leonard had cared for her – enough to ensure that she would be provided for in the event of his death – only intensified the aching sense of loss she felt. She missed him so much she could have died of it; his unobtrusive kindness, his concern, his loving presence in her life, his shoulder to cry on. She was alone again, totally alone, and the world seemed a dark and hostile place. She grew thin and tense; had nightmares and, worse, dreams where Leonard was still alive, talking with her, laughing with her; and the disappointment when she awoke and remembered was almost too much to bear.

'I can't stand it, Cindi,' she said.

'You can. You have to,' her friend replied, kind but firm. 'This is the most difficult part, love, the numbness wearing off. You've been protected until now; this is a natural reaction. Don't try and escape it. You have to go through it. Leonard's worth that, isn't he?'

'It's so hard ...'

'Oh, love, I know. I know it is. Be brave, and keep busy!'

So Annabel did, flinging herself into her work in a way that surprised even Suzy. She stayed in the office late most evenings, going through the accounts, tidying up the paperwork, interviewing new models; anything rather than go home to her empty flat and face the memories and the pain.

*

Ben Lawrence found her there one night at half-past nine, her head bent wearily over a pile of invoices. She raised her eyes to his and he saw the dark circles under them, the way her cheekbones had drawn in to make her eyes look more enormous than ever. Annabel had always been slim but now she was painfully skinny and even her hair had lost its usual bronze sheen.

'What brings you here?' she asked him.

'I saw the light when I was passing,' Ben lied. In fact, Jacqui had telephoned him and suggested he check up on Annabel, since she could get no answer from her flat. 'What are you doing here at this hour?'

'Just checking some things,' said Annabel vaguely.

'Couldn't it wait till tomorrow?' Ben's voice was gentle. Annabel shrugged. 'I suppose so, but what else can I do?'

She sounded so defeated, so utterly hopeless and dispirited, that he was alarmed.

'Come home with me, Annie. Jacqui and I were just saying how long it is since you came up to our place.'

Annabel did not protest so he brought her coat and put it around her thin shoulders. As she got up, she swayed slightly.

'How long is it since you ate?' he asked her, sharply.

She waved a vague hand. 'Not sure. This morning ... last night ...'

'Oh, Annie!'

She looked at him with huge, sorrowful eyes. 'It doesn't matter what I do, whether I eat or not.'

Ben didn't bother arguing with her. He picked her up in his arms as easily as if she had been his own little daughter, and carried her down to his waiting car. They drove up to Hampstead with Annabel slumped in the passenger seat, tears trickling weakly down her pale cheeks.

'Annie needs to eat,' said Ben briefly, helping her through into the living-room where Marie-Claude and Jacqui sat sewing. 'Can we rustle something up, do you think?'

'Of course!'

Marie-Claude went out to make sandwiches, and Jacqui poured Annabel a large brandy which brought a bit of colour back into her cheeks.

'Annie,' she said gently, 'I think you should go away.'

'Go away?' said Annabel listlessly. 'Where to? Why?'

'You're shattered,' Jacqui went on. 'You need a rest, a change, a healing time if you like. A sort of ... convalescence for your spirit.'

'If you think so.'

'I do. We all do. Don't we, Ben?'

Ben nodded.

'Somewhere sunny and warm, with no telephones to bother you, where you can relax and come to terms with things again. At the moment you are much too near everything, there are too many memories – it's no wonder you're in the state you're in!'

'Of course we can manage without you,' said Suzy firmly the next day, when Jacqui outlined her plan. 'Take three weeks off, if you like, Annie! Gillian and I will cope perfectly well here, and we'll get a temp as well.'

Annabel looked from her determined face to Jacqui's gentle one. 'All right, you win. Where shall I go?'

'Where do you fancy?' said Jacqui. 'Africa, maybe? The Seychelles? Mexico?'

'I know!' said Suzy suddenly. 'What about that hotel the *Carousel* crowd went to, on that tiny Caribbean island?'

'You mean Sainte-Marguérite?' said Jacqui. 'Oh, yes, that would be perfect. There's absolutely nothing there except sand and sea and palm trees and coral reefs, this one hotel, and a little fishing village. It's ideal!'

'Do you know the name of the hotel?' said Suzy, reaching for the phone. 'I'll call the travel agent now!'

Jacqui shook her head. 'Cathy James will have it. You'd better call her. I think you have to fly to Saint Lucia and then get a tiny one-man ferry to Sainte-Marguérite. It really is off the beaten track! How does that sound, Annie?'

'Lovely,' said Annabel, without enthusiasm. I know they want to help, she thought, touched, and I might as well go along with it. I don't care any more. It doesn't matter where I go, or what I do. Nothing matters any more.

15

The heat hit Annabel as soon as she stepped out of the plane. She stood at the top of the steps, blinking uncertainly in spite of her sunglasses. The primrose-yellow linen dress she wore, which had seemed absurdly summery in the chilly London air, now clung uncomfortably to the backs of her legs. She made her way cautiously down the steps and across to the airport building. It was cooler inside; air-conditioned, of course. Annabel handed over her passport to be checked and stood quietly waiting for her cases to be unloaded.

What am I doing here, she thought in bewilderment, looking around her at the other passengers; weary, crumpled-looking travellers like herself, their European clothes and pale faces contrasting oddly with the bright vivid colours and glowing brown skins of the local people.

'You're for Sainte-Marguérite, lady?' An elderly man, as wrinkled as an old walnut, stood beside her.

'Oh! Oh, yes, that's right.'

'Got your cases?'

'They're just coming through now.'

The driver must have been stronger than he looked because he heaved Annabel's cases across the hall and out of the building without a backward glance at her. Dumbly, Annabel followed him out.

'Am I the only one for Sainte-Marguérite?' she asked him, climbing into the back of a surprisingly smart yellow taxi. The driver grinned at her.

'Sure are. Not many people go to Sainte-Marguérite!'

That was what Annabel had been told, it seemed a million years ago. The Sunset Beach Hotel, the only one on the tiny, obscure Caribbean island, was owned by a Frenchman, a distant relative or friend of Louis Duval's, who had married a local girl. 'You'll love it, Annie!' Cathy James had told her. 'They're ever so keen to get people over there now they've done the place up, but it's still completely unspoiled. They were fantastic to us when we went there on the trip; they couldn't do enough to help! It was more like staying with friends than being in a hotel. It's just what you need, honestly!'

Annabel had smiled her remote sad smile and allowed herself to be organized into a three-week stay at the Sunset Beach. I might as well give in to them, I might as well be there as here, it doesn't matter where I am, she had thought drearily. I know they're trying to help, but it all seems so pointless.

The taxi wound its way along steep mountain roads lined with impossibly bright green trees. Here and there, through the hills, Annabel caught a glimpse of the sea, of banana plantations, of flocks of gaily-coloured parrots. It's beautiful, she thought flatly, but the feeling of total unreality persisted. There seemed to be an invisible screen between her and any emotion, any feeling, any sense of appreciation.

The road began to dip down, twisting and winding, until finally they reached a tiny port, consisting of no more than a handful of houses, dazzling white beneath the tropical sun. Two elderly fishermen in tattered white shirts and trousers sat cross-legged on the quayside, mending their nets. A tall woman in a bright orange dress strolled along, a plump brown baby on her hip and a string bag of fruit in her other hand. She smiled as Annabel got out of the taxi and stretched her cramped limbs. I need a cold drink, she thought.

Half-a-dozen small fishing-boats lay at anchor, bobbing slightly in the swell. Beside them was a little motorboat, painted blue, the kind that Annabel had often seen sailing up and down the Thames on Sunday afternoons at Windsor or Henley. A skinny dark boy wearing nothing but a pair of faded cut-off Levis emerged from it, wiping his hands on an oil-stained rag.

'You Miss Lee?' he asked her with a friendly grin.

Annabel nodded.

'Hi. I'm John, from Sunset Beach. Those your bags?'

'Yes.'

'Sling 'em over, would you? Then we can get going!'

Somewhat surprised, Annabel complied. He put his hand out to help her down and she settled herself in the stern of the tiny craft, her cases beside her. John started the engine up, and smiled at her again.

'Jeez, I did that all wrong, didn't I? I should have got out and helped you with the cases! I'll never get this right! My sister says, I don't treat our guests right, she send me back to my mum!'

Annabel's brow cleared. 'It's your sister and her husband who own the hotel?'

'Yeah, that's right. I'm helping them, but I don't do too good, do I?'

Annabel chuckled, surprising herself. 'It doesn't matter a bit!'

They moved away from the quayside and out into the open sea. Annabel trailed her hand over the side. The water was almost lukewarm, and she could see the shapes of coral beneath it. Clouds of tiny silver fish swam past her fingers and a gentle breeze lifted her hair and blew it back from her hot face. John held the wheel in one hand and turned to look at her curiously.

'You been sick? You don't look good!' he said.

Annabel sighed. 'No ... not sick, not really. I had a lot of family trouble.'

John made an odd little whistling sound through his teeth and shook his head. 'You had troubles? That's bad. That's why you came to Sainte-Marguérite, to forget your troubles?'

'I guess so.'

The boat trip took around three quarters of an hour. Then Annabel saw the shape of Sainte-Marguérite rising out of the sea ahead of them. At first she could simply see a dark blur, but gradually she could make out palm trees, tiny white houses, people, fishing-boats ...

'That's the village, Sainte-Marguérite,' said John, jerking his thumb towards the little settlement. 'Not much there, only bars, a little market, and shops. Ten more minutes now to Sunset Beach.'

They rounded a headland and Annabel gasped. There in front of them was a perfect beach, with silver sand, a tiny wooden jetty, and swaying palm-trees almost to the water's edge. The sea was so clear she could see the boat's shadow, and her own, making a dappled pattern on the sea bed. When they reached the shallows John cut the engine and leapt out into the water, tying the boat to a rusty set of steps going up to the jetty.

Annabel climbed out awkwardly and waited while John hauled her cases up on to the jetty beside her.

'You OK? Follow me!' he said, rather breathlessly.

They walked along the rough planking, across the sand and in beneath the trees. A winding path led upwards, bordered by poinsettia and hibiscus and broad-leaved plants that Annabel didn't recognize. Huge rainbow-hued butterflies fluttered past them. A few yards further on the path opened out and Annabel found herself facing a low, white-painted building. A few steps led up to the front door and at the side Annabel caught a glimpse of a patio with shady umbrellas, and the cool blue gleam of a swimming-pool. A very tall, dark woman with deep honey-coloured skin came down the steps, wearing a flowing scarlet dress and huge gold earrings. Her hands were outstretched in welcome.

'Miss Lee? Welcome to Sunset Beach! I'm Haidée Garnier. I hope you will be very happy with us!' Her voice was low and sweet with the unmistakable lilt of the Caribbean.

'Why, thank you,' said Annabel, feeling ridiculously stiff and British.

'John, I've put Miss Lee in Number Seven, so you can take her bags right over there. Miss Lee, I'd be pleased if you'd come and have a drink right away. I expect you need one, don't you? It's all ready!'

'It's very kind of you.'

Haidée smiled. 'We like to give our guests a real Sainte-Marguérite welcome! Especially when they're friends of Louis's all the way from England!'

Annabel followed her across the cool, shadowy hallway, through a comfortable-looking lounge with big French windows and out on to the patio where a tray with a big jug of something cold and inviting waited, in the shade of a sweetly-scented frangipani, thick with white and gold blossom.

'How was your journey?'

'Oh, it was all right, thank you.'

Annabel could hardly remember it. It seemed so long ago that she had waited in the noise and bustle of Heathrow with Ben and Jacqui; since Ben had kissed her and wished her better, since Jacqui had said, 'Oh, Annie, love ...' and enfolded her in a friendly hug. Ben and Jacqui, half the world away. Suzy, who would be in the cream-and-green Annabel Lee office now, making bookings, sorting out problems, chatting to Gillian ... With an effort, Annabel dragged her thoughts away. If I keep thinking about home, I'll never get to feel any different, she thought. Better to live for the moment, make the most of now.

'I'd like to go to my room,' she said, draining her glass.

'Fine. I'll show you,' Haidée smiled.

The accommodation at Sunset Beach consisted of small, self-contained bungalows set among the trees between the Clubhouse and the beach. Each had a bedsitting-room, its own shower-room, and a tiny patio. Haidée flung the shutters back and the late afternoon sun streamed in. Annabel's cases were already there, beside one of the beds.

'Everything all right?'

'It looks lovely,' said Annabel truthfully.

'I'll leave you to settle yourself in, then. Dinner's at eight!' said Haidée.

Annabel rinsed her sticky hands in the washbasin and kicked off her sandals before heaving her suitcase up on to one of the twin beds and rummaging in her handbag for her keys. It was a plain but attractive little room with white-washed walls, two beds with flower-patterned counterpanes, a wardrobe and a chest of drawers. On the patio were two cane chairs, their cushions patterned with flowered cotton to match the counterpanes, and a small table. Annabel unlocked her cases and busied herself with unpacking, hanging her clothes in the wardrobe, arranging her make-up on the chest of drawers, putting her toilet articles in the bathroom. She pulled the shutters closed for a moment and wriggled out of her creased linen dress, putting on one of her infinitely cooler and more comfortable T-shirt dresses.

She looked at her watch. It was six o'clock.

Maybe I'll have a shower, she thought, or even a dip in the pool, or explore around a bit now it's getting cooler. She yawned suddenly. Plenty of time for that tomorrow, she thought; right now I just need to put my feet up.

She lay down, folding back the flowered counterpane. The pillow was cool and smooth against her cheeks. An electric fan whirred in the roof and she watched it idly. I'll just lie down for ten minutes, she thought, then I'll wander round ...

When she came to, the shadows were lengthening and she lay for a few moments wondering where she was. Then she got up, had a quick shower, repaired her make-up and twisted her hair into a loose knot on the top of her head.

'Everything all right?' Haidée Garnier greeted her at the door to the patio. 'The dining-room is just over on the left there!'

'Everything's fine!' said Annabel. 'I had a little sleep, I'm afraid!'

'Good. Looks like we're relaxing you already!' smiled Haidée.

Annabel was shown to her table by John, now dressed somewhat incongruously in a waiter's white jacket and black trousers. He grinned cheerfully at her. 'Look pretty smart, don't I?' he said proudly.

Even Annabel, who couldn't remember enjoying a meal since before Leonard's death, was impressed by the evening meal at Sunset Beach. It was all set out on trestle tables at one side of the room and turned out to be the most extensive buffet that Annabel had ever seen. Cold meats of all kinds, shellfish, salads of every possible description, shiny green peppers and huge scarlet tomatoes stuffed with rice and beans, chicken in creamy sauce, and the fruit! Pineapples with their insides scooped out and replaced by delicious-looking fruit and nut mixtures, great bunches of bananas, mangoes, pawpaws, piled oranges and other fruits Annabel had never seen before. She could see through an archway into the kitchen where someone, presumably François Garnier himself, presided over an enormous grill. Annabel sniffed appreciatively as the scent of grilling fish and herbs floated through to her.

'Help yourself!' said Haidée, smiling. Annabel took a modest portion of fruit and salad, and returned to her table.

There didn't seem to be very many guests. An elderly couple sat over at the other side of the room; he in a pale fawn suit, she in a tight white dress. There was a family, French or Italian by the look of them, with a brood of tanned, dark-eyed children. Two men in their fifties sat at tables alone, and there was also a blue-rinsed, middle-aged lady who couldn't have looked more American if she had been waving the Stars and Stripes and singing 'Dixie'.

She went to bed early that night, and slept long and dreamlessly without taking any sleeping pills. When she awoke the next morning, the sun was high in the sky and she realized that she must have missed breakfast altogether. How long is it since I slept straight through like that? she thought in amazement. She slipped into her bikini and a cotton shirt and went up to the Clubhouse again. To her surprise, there was food available at the bar as well as coffee.

'We don't serve breakfast in the dining-room after nine-thirty but you can always get fruit and croissants here at the bar,' Haidée explained.

'That seems civilized!' said Annabel, biting into a ripe yellow peach.

When she had eaten, she wandered back along the flower-lined pathway to her bungalow beneath the jacaranda trees. She flopped down on the bed, realizing for the first time that she had absolutely *nothing* to do. Nobody was going to call her, no one was going to come and see her, there were no demands on her time at all.

I can please myself, she thought. I can swim or sunbathe, or sunbathe or swim, or explore the island a bit, or have a look at that magnificent beach, or those flowers, and that's all. Her spirits lifted, for perhaps the first time since Leonard died. I'm going to come through this, she thought, suddenly and exultantly. I'm going to learn to live again ...

The feeling of buoyant optimism didn't last, of course. There were times still when she longed for Leonard with a desperation that was almost a physical pain, but they were fewer and fewer. As the long, slow days drifted by, she found that she could think of him and smile, and she knew with an instinct stronger than reason that that was how Leonard would have wanted it to be. She grew brown and well and her face lost its hollow, haunted look. Her days fell into a simple, lazy routine; to the beach every morning after breakfast to sunbathe, and then a dip in the warm turquoise sea and a shower before lunch. In the afternoon she had a siesta when the sun was at its hottest, and then a walk in the cool tropical forest, where birds and insects were her only companions and the sun only occasionally filtered through the matted, dense foliage.

A couple of times, Annabel wandered along the beach to the village. There was a street market, with piles of exotic fruit and vegetables, dubious-looking meat, gleaming fish sold straight from the back of the boat, lengths of bright dyed cotton, cheap clothes, woven straw hats and bags, and the ubiquitous Coca-Cola. Small dark-skinned children chattered and giggled at Annabel, staring at her round-eyed and scampering away when she stopped and tried to make friends with them. One little girl, bolder than the rest, came up to her as she sat on the harbour wall watching the comings and goings. She was a skinny child of perhaps seven or eight, in a too-small pink cotton dress, with her hair braided into dozens of tiny plaits.

'Hello, lady, I'm Mary,' she said solemnly.

Annabel smiled at her.

'You don't speak English?' the child asked anxiously.

'I speak English!' said Annabel, laughing, and the little girl laughed too.

'You stayin' at the hotel?'

'That's right.'

'You havin' a holiday? Me, I live here all the time!'

'Aren't you lucky! I wish I did!'

'Where do you live?'

'I live in England. That's a long, long way away over the sea.'

The child scrambled to her feet. 'I got things to do,' she said mysteriously. 'You come by this way again and I'll see you then!'

'I'll do that,' Annabel promised.

The little girl scampered off to rejoin her friends, clearly reassuring them that the lady wasn't too fearsome after all. From then on, whenever Annabel was in the village she found herself with an entourage of small, fascinated black children who seemed to want nothing more than to look at her and stroke her hair.

She gave Mary a red cotton scarf that she'd found at the bottom of her suitcase and this seemed to increase the little girl's status among her friends to a fantastic degree. She wore it all the time; tied round her head, loosely knotted at her neck, or once tucked into the waistband of her skirt. In some way, Mary's easy acceptance and, yes, friendship warmed Annabel's heart in a way that adult companionship wouldn't have done. There were no questions, no problems, no demands on either side, and Annabel found herself wishing she could take Mary home with her and see London and England through the honest and surprisingly perceptive eyes of an eight-year-old Caribbean child.

She slept, too. Annabel, who for years had managed on six or seven hours' sleep and was frequently bothered by nightmares and insomnia; who had needed strong sleeping tablets to knock her out ever since Leonard's death, now found herself sleeping the clock round with no trouble at all. It must be true what they say about fresh air and exercise, she thought vaguely, in the hazy, almost mindless contentment that this new way of life had brought her. I'm out in the open air from morning till night, I do all that walking, all that swimming – that's why I'm not getting fat in spite of all the food I'm eating! Because her appetite was improving too, with gentle encouragement from Haidée and endless temptation from François in the shape of fruit flans, cocktails spiced with rum and nutmeg, and pastries so light they melted on the tongue.

'You spoil me!' she had protested, laughing, when François presented her with yet another irresistible morsel.

'Spoil? I don't understand!' said François, with a very Gallic shrug. His English, Annabel had noticed, tended to desert him when he wanted it to! What could she do but smile, and give in?

*

'We have a new group coming next week. Americans,' Haidée told her at the end of her second week on Sainte-Marguérite. Annabel wrinkled her nose, imagining a party of loud, camera-toting tourists invading her island paradise. Oh dear, she thought, I know they want to encourage tourism here, and I'm sure it would be good for the people, but it's so lovely as it is I don't want it ever to change and get spoiled! She had seen next to nothing of her fellow guests at Sunset Beach. The French family had left at the end of her first week and been replaced by a wealthy-looking couple with a pasty-faced teenage daughter. One of the businessmen had gone, too, and two young men, whom John told her were scuba-diving en-thusiasts, had arrived. They were both young, tanned and good-looking, and the first time they had appeared in the dining-room the pasty-faced teenager had brightened up considerably, but since discovering that they spent the time from sunrise to sunset at sea she had relapsed into bored indifference again. I suppose there's not much here for a kid like that, thought Annabel, torn between sympathy and ex-asperation. No night life, no handsome life guards, no discos ... thank Heavens!

That evening, at dinner-time, she was surprised to see the middle-aged American lady she had noticed on her first evening threading her way across the room towards her, a cup of coffee balanced precariously in one hand.

'Do you mind if I join you, my dear?' she said, smiling pleasantly at Annabel, who thought at once that two weeks ago the last thing she would have wanted was this lady's company. After a fortnight of virtual isolation, though, the idea of conversation was definitely appealing. She smiled back.

'Please do!'

'Thank you.'

She settled down, putting her coffee cup on the table and a huge handbag brimming over with spectacle cases, knitting, paperbacks and other paraphernalia on the floor beside her.

'Are you enjoying your holiday?'

'Oh, yes. Yes!' said Annabel. Enjoyment didn't seem quite the word, she thought. It had been more like convalescence, revitalization, a healing period for her battered spirit.

'You look all the better for it, if I may say so,' the woman said, peering over her glasses at Annabel. 'I noticed you when you first arrived. I said to myself, now there's a girl who's had a bad time. A very bad time. Am I right?'

'Well, yes,' said Annabel uncertainly.

The woman patted her hand. 'Oh, excuse me, my dear, I didn't introduce myself. I'm Berta Barnes, from Atlanta, Georgia.'

'Annabel Lee, from London,' said Annabel automatically, and Miss – or Mrs – Barnes frowned.

'Annabel Lee? Like the Edgar Allan Poe poem? Well, isn't that romantic? Your mother must have had real taste to give you a beautiful name like that!'

Annabel laughed, recognizing a kindred spirit underneath the soft Southern drawl, the rhinestoned spectacles and unlikely mauve dress. 'Actually, I was christened Anne,' she confided. 'I used to do modelling, though, and when I went into it I decided I would need a name people would remember.'

'Well, it's real pretty,' said Berta Barnes. 'I guess I should have come over and introduced myself before but, you know, I didn't want to seem too pushy. We have a tendency to that fault, we Americans, don't you think?'

'I have some very nice American friends. I'd never call them pushy!' said Annabel loyally.

'Oh, you have American friends?'

'Yes. Actually, the girl I share my flat – sorry, my apartment – with in London is an air stewardess from San Francisco, and she's a darling!'

'You're from London, England? You know, I always wanted to see London. My husband, the late Mr Barnes, he was over in England in World War Two and he spoke so highly of the people there. We planned to go back one day but,' she sighed, 'it wasn't to be, unfortunately!'

Annabel felt a pang of sympathy.

'I have a nerve, don't I?' continued Mrs Barnes. 'A lovely young woman like you can't be all alone for no reason. Did you leave your husband at home ... or no, you said you have a room-mate. Now let me guess ... you've just said goodbye to a beau, as we used to call them in my day. Am I right?'

Annabel drew a deep breath. 'Not quite,' she said. 'I was engaged to be married, and then he was killed in a car crash.'

It was the first time she had told anyone here. It hurt, but not with the dull desperate ache she had felt before; just a clean wound that she knew would heal with time and care and courage.

Mrs Barnes was looking at her, her eyes round with horror. She recovered her composure, and patted Annabel's hand again. 'Oh, my dear. Oh, how dreadful of me. I'm so sorry ...'

Annabel shook her head. 'My friends made me come here. They said it would help me.'

'And has it helped?'

'More than I could ever have imagined.'

Dear Jacqui, she thought, dear Ben, dear reliable Suzy, Cindi with her worried face and loving sympathy. I'll be seeing them again in a week, and they'll help me pick myself up and start again ...

'It's so peaceful and beautiful here,' she went on, 'and the Garniers have been so kind.'

Mrs Barnes nodded. 'I know. They're wonderful people. You know, Annabel – may I call you Annabel? – when I lost my dear husband, I thought I'd never smile or laugh or care ever again, but I do! We had so much love that it would be – unfair – to him if I shut myself off from the world and went on grieving the way I wanted to do at first.'

Annabel swallowed the lump in her throat. 'I know. My fiancé, Leonard, always took such good care of me I can't believe there's nothing left!'

'Remember the good times, Annabel. He would want it that way!'

Annabel wept a little, in bed that night, but they were gentle, healing tears, and when she got up the next morning she felt totally at peace with herself and the world around her. She went to the beach straightaway, tossed off her shirt, and slipped into the clear water. She swam around lazily for a few moments, wondering whether it might be possible to take a boat out across the bay to explore some of the coral reefs. Maybe those two scuba-divers would take me, she thought idly. I'll ask them at dinner-time.

After her swim she popped back to her bungalow to rinse the seawater from her hair and skin. She pinned her hair up again and looked critically at her lightly-tanned body in the mirror. Not bad, she thought. One more week and I'll be a really good colour. Being auburn-haired and fair-skinned, Annabel never got a deep tan, but she was lucky in that she didn't burn. Her eyes looked a deeper green against her honey-coloured skin and the sun had brought out her few freckles.

She grinned at her reflection, smothered Ambre Solaire over her shoulders and legs, and set off back to the beach. It's such a good feeling, lying in the sun, she thought drowsily, reaching round to untie the strap of her bikini and feeling the sun beating down on her shoulder-blades. Lazily, she picked up a handful of the white sand and let it trickle through her fingers. It's not really white, she thought, it's grey, and yellow, and brown, and—

Squinting through half-closed eyes, she saw a man in the distance, walking down the beach towards her. He seemed to be carrying something. Must be one of the scuba-divers, she thought vaguely, and sat up, clutching her bikini top, intending to ask him if she could hitch a lift in his boat. The sun was right behind him so she couldn't see his face, but there was something familiar about the way he walked. She frowned, puzzled. It couldn't be one of the scuba-divers; they were both dark and this man had quite light-coloured hair. As he came nearer, she saw that he was carrying a camera, and not snorkelling equipment ... and then Annabel knew.

He had seen her. He stopped. She couldn't see the expression on his face.

'Annie? Annabel?' His voice was incredulous.

It was Richard.

16

Annabel was so shocked that she could only stare at him. He laughed uneasily. 'Annie? It *is* you, isn't it?'

She was still fumbling ineffectually with her bikini strap.

In one deft movement he reached over and fastened it for her. At the touch of his fingers she pulled away, and he frowned.

'What are you doing here?' she managed to gasp.

He sat down beside her on the sand. 'I'm on a trip,' he explained gently. 'A fashion trip with *Chérie* magazine in New York. D'you know it?'

Annabel nodded. *Chérie* was a prestige glossy which was much admired in England. Then she remembered. 'Haidée – Madame Garnier – told me there were some Americans coming, but I thought she meant tourists.'

'Well, no. It's us. Myself, my assistant, the Fashion Editor and her assistant, two models and a hairdresser.'

Oh, no, Annabel thought, two models. I wonder if he's brought his girlfriend, the fabulous Leonora, the toast of New York. I can't bear it. It isn't fair, just when I was beginning to feel good again, at peace with myself. Why did this have to happen? I can't go through it all again.

She scrambled to her feet. 'I must go!' she said wildly.

'Go? Go where?'

Anywhere, she thought, anywhere those much too perceptive grey eyes can't see me and read my mind. I've got over you, Richard Redding, I won't let you tear my heart apart a second time.

'To get ready for lunch!' she said.

'Annie, it's only a quarter to eleven!'

She looked at him dumbly.

'Don't run away from me, Annabel!'

Her chin went up. He was right. Annabel Lee was more than a match for any man. She wouldn't run away; there was nowhere to go, anyway. She'd stay and face him out, him and his trendy New York lady with her cover-girl face and her movie rôles. Probably she wouldn't see much of them anyway, since they'd be working most of the day. She sat down beside him again and smiled a brittle, meaningless social smile.

'It *is* a surprise seeing you again!' she said. 'How long are you here for?'

'Just four days, unfortunately,' he said, looking around him. 'I could do with staying longer. It looks beautiful!'

'Oh, it is,' she assured him brightly. 'I've been here two weeks already and I fly home on Sunday.'

He raised his eyebrows. 'Three weeks' holiday? It's not like you to be so self-indulgent, Annie!'

'I needed a rest,' she said briefly.

So he doesn't know about Leonard, she thought. She gave Richard a quick, sidelong glance. He hadn't changed, not to look at, anyway. The same faded jeans, the same untidy hair; a deeper tan, perhaps, and more self-assurance, but the same long eyelashes and strong hands ... and the same smile ... oh, stop, dear God, don't let me remember!

'I hear you've done pretty well in New York!' she said conversationally.

Was it her imagination, or did he look faintly bewildered? 'Yes, I can't complain.'

'You've done TV chat shows, and *Vogue*, and things.'

'How do you know that?'

'Ben told me.'

'Oh, yes, Ben. It was a shame I missed him when he was in town. I work a pretty tight schedule these days anyway.'

She noticed he pronounced it in the American way.

'But how about you, Annie? How are things with you? Still the same?'

Annabel realized with a shock of surprise that it was a scant five months since Richard had left London. It seemed like half a lifetime. The lonely weeks after he had gone, the pain of missing him, the leap of her heart when Ben came back from New York with news of him ... and then the news, and Leonora. Her engagement, Leonard's death. The end of her world, or part of it.

'Yes,' she lied, 'everything's the same.'

'How are Ben and Jacqui? How's the job?'

'They're fine. Everything's OK at Annabel Lee, too.'

Her eyes met his, and all her brave resolutions faltered. Oh, Richard, she thought, there's so much that has changed, and so much that hasn't ...

'Shouldn't you be working?' she said briskly, 'if you only have four days?'

He looked at his watch. 'We said we'd try and do some shots this afternoon and give the girls the chance of a rest this morning,' he said. 'I'm supposed to be looking for good locations, actually. I couldn't believe it when I saw you sitting there. I thought I was seeing things!'

'Thanks!'

'You know I didn't mean –' he said abruptly, and stopped.

She got up. 'Well, there's no shortage of locations. There's the beach, the jungle, the pool, the Clubhouse, the village ... I heard about this place from Cathy James at *Carousel*. They were here a few months ago.'

'It's like Paradise, isn't it?' Richard said thoughtfully, watching a bright scarlet humming-bird dart back into the lush greenery of the forest.

'Perfect. There aren't even many creepy-crawlies.'

'That so? I must tell Sandy,' he said. 'She's one of the models and she was scared stiff the place would be crawling with snakes and scorpions and all kinds of nasty things.'

'Haidée said there are snakes, but I haven't seen one,' said Annabel, her heart beating fast. 'Are they nice, the models?'

'Oh, they seem OK. You know what models are,' said Richard casually. 'They seemed to spend most of the flight discussing the best way to get rid of split ends with Victor, the hairdresser. I don't think we'll have any trouble with them.'

So he hasn't brought Leonora, thought Annabel, relieved. At least I won't have to meet her and be polite to her!

'I'm going back to my bungalow,' she said. 'I'll see you later!'

'Yes, see you, Annie!'

She lay on her bed, watching the electric fan whirring round in the roof, and tried to think. How did she feel about Richard now, after all the time that had passed and all that she had been through since he had left for New York? Did she love him, hate him, resent him for disturbing her hard-won equilibrium?

'I'd like to think we could still be friends, Annabel!' he had said, at her flat in London, the night before he left. Could she be friends with him, or at least seem to be, even for four days? Friendship seemed a pale, poor thing, after love ... but then, he had never said he loved her, she remembered bleakly, not in all the time they had been together, not even when they lay in each other's arms, sleepy after making love.

I won't think about it. Four days, only four days, and he'll be gone, and I can start again.

She took particular care with her hair and clothes when she dressed for lunch, slipping her white Swiss caftan on over her bikini, and putting on make-up for the first time since she had been on Sainte-Marguérite. When she got up to the bar, the party from New York were already there, sipping big glasses of Haidée's special rum punch.

'Annabel! Come and say hello!' said Richard cheerfully. He introduced her, she noticed, as 'a friend of mine from London'. 'And this is Donna, from *Chérie*, and Tricia her assistant,' he went on. 'Stevie works with me, and that's Victor, and these are our models, Sandy and Maribeth. Annabel runs a model agency in London.'

'Oh, really?' Maribeth, a slim brunette who reminded Annabel a bit of Cindi, smiled at her. 'Is it easy to start up on your own in London?'

'Well, I wouldn't say it was easy,' said Annabel, 'but if you have the right girls, and the right backing' – she swallowed suddenly, remembering Leonard – 'and you can survive the first few months till you're established, you're generally OK.'

'Annabel's being modest,' Richard smiled. 'Hers is one of the best agencies in London. Everyone says so!'

And so it should be, considering the sacrifices I've made for it, Annabel thought with some bitterness.

'It must be a big responsibility, though, a business of your own,' said the other model, Sandy, who was clearly younger and shyer than Maribeth.

'Yes, it is, but I enjoy it. I used to model myself but I like this a lot better.'

'And you come to places like Sainte-Marguérite on holiday instead of to work!' said the Fashion Editor, a plain-faced but pleasant-looking woman in her mid-thirties.

'Well, there is that!' said Annabel, and everyone laughed.

After lunch, they were all sitting enjoying their coffee on the poolside patio when Mrs Barnes came puffing up to Annabel. She settled down in her chair, shedding belongings right, left and centre, and smiled amiably round at everyone.

'Oh my, new friends,' she said. 'Yankees too, I'll bet!'

Annabel introduced her to the team from *Chérie* and then, with only a very slight tremor in her voice, to Richard. 'An old friend of mine from England, who works in New York now,' she said.

'Someone you know? Why, now, Annabel, isn't that a coincidence?'

'It certainly is,' said Richard gravely. 'I met Annabel down on the beach and I couldn't believe it was really her!'

'She's looking well, isn't she?' said Berta Barnes fondly.

'Yes, she looks great.' He did not look at Annabel.

'If you'll excuse us,' Donna said, 'we have to iron some clothes for this afternoon's session.'

They drifted away and were soon followed by Maribeth, murmuring that she wanted Victor to roll up her hair, and an apprehensive-looking Sandy.

Annabel yawned suddenly. 'Mmm. I'm getting used to my little siesta after lunch,' she said lightly. 'I'll see you all later!'

Mrs Barnes and Richard watched Annabel for a moment as she walked down the path through the trees towards her bungalow.

'Annabel's a dear girl,' she said, sipping her glass of iced punch. 'I've become very fond of her.'

Richard smiled politely.

'I'm glad to see her looking so well. She looked like a washed-out rag when she came here two weeks ago, poor thing.'

'She works too hard. It's an occupational hazard!' he said abruptly.

'Well, yes, and then that terrible tragedy ...'

'Tragedy?'

'Losing her fiancé that way.'

'Her fiancé?'

Berta Barnes looked at him. 'You didn't know?'

At his stunned expression, she covered her mouth with a plump, beringed hand. 'You didn't ... oh, my, I've said the wrong thing! But Annabel said you were an old friend, and I just assumed ...'

'I've been in New York since January, and Annabel and I have rather lost touch,' said Richard bleakly. 'I'm sorry, Mrs Barnes, but you'd better tell me!'

'Well,' she said carefully, 'the reason Annabel came on this vacation was to help her ... adjust, I guess you'd say, to losing

165

her fiancé. He was killed in an auto accident.'

'I see.'

'Gee, I'm sorry . . . sorry to be the one to tell you, I mean!
You knew him, I guess, if you were a friend of Annabel's.
He sounded like a fine man, Leonard. I guess Annabel
couldn't find the words to tell you herself. I know she doesn't
like to talk about it, that's why I was so flattered she confided
in me. I know what it is to lose a dear one, you see . . gee,
what can I say?'

Richard seemed to come to life. 'It's all right, Mrs Barnes.
I'm glad you told me. You're right, it would have been hard
for Annabel to tell me herself.'

'He must have been a fine man.'

'Yes. Yes, a fine man.'

Richard set off along the path to Annabel's bungalow, and
then stopped, abruptly, when he heard Stevie's voice behind
him. They were due to begin shooting soon, and he needed
more than ten snatched minutes with Annabel, now that he
knew. He turned round. 'OK, Stevie, I'm coming!' he said.

It began to look to Richard, over the next forty-eight
hours, as if Annabel was deliberately avoiding him. That
first evening he waited for an opportunity to speak to her,
but was called away by Donna, the Fashion Editor, who
wanted to discuss the next day's shooting. This took longer
than he expected, and when he returned to the bar Haidée
told him that Annabel had gone to bed. The next day, Richard
began working at eight in the morning, before Annabel got
up. They decided to shoot around the village and the harbour
in the afternoon, and discovered Sainte-Marguérite's one and
only restaurant, where the proprietor was so thrilled at the
prospect of appearing in an American magazine that he insisted on offering them all dinner 'on the house'! The next
day he hurried to Annabel's bungalow after breakfast, but it
was empty. He asked John casually if he knew where she was,
and was told that Annabel had gone out in the boat with
the scuba-divers, saying she wouldn't be back till nightfall.

She *is* avoiding me, Richard thought.

Annabel, out in the middle of the bay in Pete and José's glass-bottomed boat, smiled to herself. He's going on Friday, she thought, he's going back to New York and Leonora, and I'll never see him again. I'm me, I'm strong, I'll survive. I don't need anyone. She made herself concentrate on the rainbow-coloured underwater world beneath the boat. Out here the water was deep indigo blue, sometimes green, and countless multi-coloured fish darted among the coral reefs. José had offered to teach her scuba-diving, but she was content to borrow a snorkel and mask and swim lazily along just below the surface of the ocean, fascinated by this strange silent world with its bubbles and ripples and waving fronds, its shells and sea-urchins and oddly-shaped branched coral, sometimes red, sometimes grey or bronze or silvery, always changing with the ebb and flow of the tide. Once, much to her amusement, a couple of luminous yellow and blue fish swam up and inspected her curiously, for all the world as if they were asking each other what this strange, golden-brown sea-creature with the trailing red hair could be.

It was quite dark when the boat drew up at the hotel jetty. Annabel thanked Pete and José, and hurried to her bungalow, where she slept without dreaming.

Thursday, she knew, was Richard's last day. She met him at the Clubhouse at lunch-time.

'Hi there,' she said, smiling. 'How's it going?'

'Annabel,' he said, catching her arm, 'I've got to talk to you!'

She raised her eyebrows. Just then, Donna called 'Richard! We're ready!' and she heard him swear under his breath.

'Can I see you tonight?' he said urgently.

'Sure, why not?'

'Richard, are you coming?'

He looked as if he was going to say something else, but in the end he simply shook his head, grabbed his Nikon and followed Donna, Tricia and the two models. Annabel closed her eyes, trying to recapture some of the serenity she had felt in the boat. I'm strong, she repeated, as if the words were a lucky charm.

He joined her after dinner as she sat on the patio with a rum punch. 'Look, Annie,' he said awkwardly, 'we can't talk here. Come down to the beach with me!'

Her eyes were wide and defenceless for a moment, and then she said quietly, 'All right,' picked up her glass, and followed him. He was striding ahead so quickly that she almost had to run to catch up. Her evening sandals sank uncomfortably into the soft sand, and she sat down on a tussock of rough grass, her arms round her knees. The sun was just dipping down into a suddenly silver sea, and the sky was streaked and barred with the colours of sunset; rose and gold, crimson and flame. Far out across the bay the last fishing-boats made their way home, and from along the beach came the low, sweet sound of a woman's voice, singing.

'Well?' said Annabel.

'Oh, Annie,' said Richard, 'why didn't you tell me?'

'Tell you what?'

'About Leonard . . . why you came here!'

'Berta Barnes must have told you,' said Annabel flatly.

'Don't blame her,' said Richard. 'She thought I knew. Why didn't you tell me?'

'Because I couldn't.'

'You told Mrs Barnes, though!'

'Yes. She helped me. She's very sweet.'

'You haven't answered my question!'

She stood up suddenly, furious. 'Why should you care? You've got everything you ever wanted, you're a big star in New York, everyone wants to know you. I was just someone you left behind on the way up!'

'Annabel, you know that's not true!'

'Do I?'

'You were the one who said it was better to make a clean break!'

She was silent.

'I told you I'd come back. I wanted to write to you –'

'Then why didn't you?'

'Because you told me you didn't want me to,' he answered patiently. 'But look, Annabel, I want to say how sorry I was to hear about Leonard. I know how much he meant to you.'

'Did Mrs Barnes tell you we were engaged?'

'Yes. Yes, she did.'

'She didn't tell you when we got engaged, though, did she?' she said bitterly.

'When you got engaged?' he echoed, bewildered.

'Yes. It was after Ben came back from New York, and told me about you and Leonora. I was up at Leonard's place that night and he asked me to marry him, and I said I would!'

'Ben told you about me and Leonora?'

'Don't keep repeating everything I say!' She was almost shouting.

'Sssh,' he said. 'Hush, Annie, listen. Ben's been reading too many gossip columns. It's true I took Leonora Field out a few times, and it was at the time I did the TV shows so there were photographers everywhere, and we were seen at a couple of showbiz parties, but there was never anything more to it than that! I mean, Leo's a nice kid and a great model, I like her, but that's as far as it goes. She's seventeen years old, for heaven's sake! Also, she comes from California and she was kind of lonely as a newcomer to Manhattan, so we had that much in common. I hear she's dating that new teen-idol now, the one who made the roller-disco record, anyway. But we were never lovers, Annie, not in any sense!'

'But there must have been girls ...' Annabel said doubtfully.

He made a small, impatient movement. 'Oh, Christ, yes, of course there were girls. What did you expect? Didn't you go out with anyone, after I'd gone?'

'Yes ... yes, I suppose so.'

He turned to her, almost violently. 'There were girls,' he said through clenched teeth, 'but I'll tell you this much. They were nothing, nothing, I can't even remember their names. You got under my skin, Annabel Lee. You were round every corner, you were in the air I breathed and the music I heard and the things I ate and drank. When I went to sleep at night, you were there in my dreams. I could smell you and taste you and feel you in my bones. The other girls were like ghosts, shadows, reflections, because even when I made love to them I could only see you!'

'I know,' she whispered. 'I know, Richard. It was like that for me, too.'

He looked straight into her eyes. 'When you've had the best, it's hard to settle for anything less,' he said softly.

They were standing very close together, but only their fingertips touched. Slowly, very slowly, he bent his head down to touch her trembling mouth with his. It was a strange kiss, quite without passion and yet infinitely tender, and it stirred Annabel to the depths of her soul. She felt weak, defenceless, open like a parched flower under the first few drops of rain as he parted her lips with his tongue and the sweet, familiar ache began ...

Oh, I'd forgotten, she thought, dazed and helpless with love, and her hands went round his neck, her fingertips exploring his skin as if she were blind and needed to know his body again, to reassure herself that he was real.

It was like coming home. It was like finding her other self, so long sought, so eagerly awaited, the answer to her loneliness for ever. I love him, she thought, I've always loved him, and the rest were all pale shadows. Oh, Richard ...

They broke apart, smiling foolishly, as if they had been offered too much after the long deprivation and they wanted to savour it slowly and enjoy it bit by bit. He ran his hands over her arms and shoulders, nuzzling her softly, licking her ears, touching and stroking, gentling her as she remembered seeing him gentle Cleo, her kitten.

'I can't lose you again,' he murmured.

She shook her head, too overwhelmed by emotion to speak.

'It *will* be all right,' he said, holding her hand tightly in his. 'It will, love. We have to be together, you and I.'

She found her voice at last. 'It won't be easy,' she said. 'I can't give up Annabel Lee, and you can't give up photography, but even when we're apart we'll be together.'

'Of course we will,' he said. 'I don't know how I ever thought I could do without you! I was always so proud and so independent, and I was never going to let any woman get through to me and limit my freedom!'

She giggled. 'I know. I can remember you saying that, Richard, and the awful thing was I agreed with you! Freedom's just another word to describe loneliness, though. Loving doesn't stop you being free, anyway. We'll be free together!'

They sat beneath the palm trees, their arms around each other as though, having found each other at last, they couldn't bear to be apart.

'Love, I *have* to go back to New York tomorrow, though I'd give anything to be able to stay with you,' he began.

'I know. It's all right. We'll just have to face the fact that work is going to keep us apart sometimes,' she said. 'There are letters, though, and there's always the telephone, and visits. Ben does it all the time!'

'Good old Ben. If it hadn't been for him, we might never have met,' said Richard, idly picking a hibiscus blossom and tucking it into the neckline of Annabel's dress.

She shivered. 'That's an awful thought!'

He looked at her seriously. 'Annabel, there's something I really have to say. It's about Leonard ...'

'Don't. There's no need.'

'But there is. When Mrs Barnes told me he'd been killed, I felt ... guilty, as if I was responsible in some way. He loved you very much, didn't he?'

She nodded.

'Did he ... I mean ... did you ever tell him about me?'

She shook her head. 'No. No, I never did. I once thought about it, when it looked as if things were getting serious between us but he ... I don't know, he seemed to be avoiding the subject and I couldn't ... I didn't know what to say in the end. Cindi said I shouldn't tell him, anyway. I sometimes thought he must have known, or at least suspected, but ... I don't know. He was a fantastic person, Richard. He just accepted me, exactly the way I was. I did love him. I would never have said I'd marry him if I hadn't thought I could make him happy, but ... it was different.'

'Of course it was. Whoever said there was only one kind of love?'

'You do understand, don't you?'

'I understand. I don't want to take away any part of you that was Leonard's, and I should be grateful to him, too, for taking such good care of you.'

'Oh, he did. He was like a father, brother, best friend and favourite uncle, all rolled into one!'

'You'll miss him still.'

She nodded tremulously. 'I try to remember something Cindi said to me.'

'What's that?'

'That Leonard was a happy man when he ... when he died, and that not everyone could say that. I felt guilty too, Richard, until Cindi told me that.'

His hand tightened on hers. 'Well, it's just you and me now, kid.'

Her eyes were suspiciously bright, but she managed a smile. 'We'll make it, Richard. I know we will!'

He got up, and pulled her to her feet to stand beside him. It was almost dark, and across the bay the lights of Sainte-Marguérite flickered. A gentle breeze whispered in the palm trees above their heads, and the air was heavy with the scent of tropical flowers. He held her close.

'There's something else, Annie!'

'What's that?'

His eyes were dark, fathomless.

'I love you,' he said simply.

He bent to kiss her, and as he did so the hibiscus flower fell off her dress and lay unnoticed on the sand between them. As they turned to go, hand in hand, she saw it.

'Look,' she said. 'If I throw it in the sea, will that mean I'll come back to Sainte-Marguérite one day?'

'Try it,' he said, smiling. 'Try it and see!'

She picked the flower up and flung it as far as she could into the inky water. Richard slipped his arm around her shoulders and, together, they watched it rise and fall and turn in the moonlight; a tiny, fragile symbol of human hope on the dark and shining sea.

FICTION

GENERAL

- [ ] Stand on It — Stroker Ace — 95p
- [ ] Chains — Justin Adams — £1.25
- [ ] The Master Mechanic — I. G. Broat — £1.50
- [ ] Wyndward Passion — Norman Daniels — £1.35
- [ ] Abingdon's — Michael French — £1.25
- [ ] The Moviola Man — Bill and Colleen Mahan — £1.25
- [ ] Running Scared — Gregory Mcdonald — 85p
- [ ] Gossip — Marc Olden — £1.25
- [ ] The Sounds of Silence — Judith Richards — £1.00
- [ ] Summer Lightning — Judith Richards — £1.00
- [ ] The Hamptons — Charles Rigdon — £1.35
- [ ] The Affair of Nina B. — Simmel — 95p
- [ ] The Berlin Connection — Simmel — £1.50
- [ ] The Cain Conspiracy — Simmel — £1.20
- [ ] Double Agent—Triple Cross — Simmel — £1.35
- [ ] Celestial Navigation — Anne Tyler — £1.00
- [ ] Earthly Possessions — Anne Tyler — 95p
- [ ] Searching for Caleb — Anne Tyler — £1.00

WESTERN   BLADE SERIES

- [ ] No. 1   The Indian Incident — Matt Chisholm — 75p
- [ ] No. 2   The Tucson Conspiracy — Matt Chisholm — 75p
- [ ] No. 3   The Laredo Assignment — Matt Chisholm — 75p
- [ ] No. 4   The Pecos Manhunt — Matt Chisholm — 75p
- [ ] No. 5   The Colorado Virgins — Matt Chisholm — 85p
- [ ] No. 6   The Mexican Proposition — Matt Chisholm — 75p
- [ ] No. 7   The Arizona Climax — Matt Chisholm — 85p
- [ ] No. 8   The Nevada Mustang — Matt Chisholm — 85p

WAR

- [ ] Jenny's War — Jack Stoneley — £1.25
- [ ] The Killing-Ground — Elleston Trevor — £1.10

NAVAL HISTORICAL

- [ ] The Sea of the Dragon — R. T. Aundrews — 95p
- [ ] Ty-Shan Bay — R. T. Aundrews — 95p
- [ ] HMS Bounty — John Maxwell — £1.00
- [ ] The Baltic Convoy — Showell Styles — 95p
- [ ] Mr. Fitton's Commission — Showell Styles — 85p

FILM/TV TIE-IN

- [ ] American Gigolo — Timothy Harris — 95p
- [ ] Meteor — E. H. North and F. Coen — 95p
- [ ] Driver — Clyde B. Phillips — 80p

SCIENCE FICTION

- [ ] The Mind Thing — Fredric Brown — 90p
- [ ] Strangers — Gardner Dozois — 95p
- [ ] Project Barrier — Daniel F. Galouye — 80p
- [ ] Beyond the Barrier — Damon Knight — 80p
- [ ] Clash by Night — Henry Kuttner — 95p
- [ ] Fury — Henry Kuttner — 80p
- [ ] Mutant — Henry Kuttner — 90p
- [ ] Drinking Sapphire Wine — Tanith Lee — £1.25
- [ ] Journey — Marta Randall — £1.00
- [ ] The Lion Game — James H. Schmitz — 70p
- [ ] The Seed of Earth — Robert Silverberg — 80p
- [ ] The Silent Invaders — Robert Silverberg — 80p
- [ ] City of the Sun — Brian M. Stableford — 85p
- [ ] Critical Threshold — Brian M. Stableford — 75p
- [ ] The Florians — Brian M. Stableford — 80p
- [ ] Wildeblood's Empire — Brian M. Stableford — 80p
- [ ] A Touch of Strange — Theodore Sturgeon — 85p

FICTION

CRIME/ADVENTURE/SUSPENSE

☐ The Organization	David Anthony	90p
☐ Stud Game	David Anthony	95p
☐ Five Pieces of Jade	John Ball	85p
☐ Siege	Peter Cave	£1.15
☐ The Execution	Oliver Crawford	90p
☐ The Ransom Commando	James Grant	95p
☐ The Rose Medallion	James Grant	90p
☐ Barracuda	Irving A. Greenfield	95p
☐ The Halo Jump	Alistair Hamilton	£1.00
☐ The Desperate Hours	Joseph Hayes	95p
☐ A Game for the Living	Patricia Highsmith	95p
☐ The Blunderer	Patricia Highsmith	95p
☐ Those Who Walk Away	Patricia Highsmith	95p
☐ The Tremor of Forgery	Patricia Highsmith	80p
☐ The Two Faces of January	Patricia Highsmith	95p
☐ The Heir	Christopher Keane	£1.00
☐ Cranmer	Steve Knickmeyer	90p
☐ The Golden Grin	Colin Lewis	£1.00
☐ Confess, Fletch	Gregory Mcdonald	90p
☐ Fletch	Gregory Mcdonald	90p
☐ Flynn	Gregory Mcdonald	95p
☐ To Kill a Jogger	Jon Messmann	95p
☐ Pandora Man	Kerry Newcomb and Frank Schaefer	£1.25
☐ Sigmet Active	Thomas Page	£1.10
☐ The Jericho Commandment	James Patterson	£1.00
☐ Games	Bill Pronzini	85p
☐ Crash Landing	Mark Regan	95p
☐ The Mole	Dan Sherman	95p
☐ Swann	Dan Sherman	£1.00
☐ The Peking Pay-Off	Ian Stewart	90p
☐ The Seizing of Singapore	Ian Stewart	£1.00
☐ Place of the Dawn	Gordon Taylor	90p
☐ Judas Cross	Jeffrey M. Wallmann	90p
☐ Rough Deal	Walter Winward	85p
☐ The Ten-Tola Bars	Burton Wohl	90p

HISTORICAL ROMANCE/ROMANCE/SAGA

☐ Flowers of Fire	Stephanie Blake	£1.00
☐ So Wicked My Desire	Stephanie Blake	£1.50
☐ Morgana	Marie Buchanan	£1.35
☐ The Enchanted Land	Jude Deveraux	£1.50
☐ Mystic Rose	Patricia Gallagher	£1.25
☐ Alinor	Roberta Gellis	£1.20
☐ Gilliane	Roberta Gellis	£1.00
☐ Joanna	Roberta Gellis	£1.25
☐ Roselynde	Roberta Gellis	£1.20
☐ Love's Scarlet Banner	Fiona Harrowe	£1.00
☐ Lily of the Sun	Sandra Heath	95p
☐ Daneclere	Pamela Hill	£1.25
☐ Strangers' Forest	Pamela Hill	£1.00
☐ Royal Mistress	Patricia Campbell Horton	£1.50
☐ The Tall One	Barbara Jefferis	£1.00
☐ Captive Bride	Johanna Lindsey	£1.00
☐ The Flight of the Dove	Catherine MacArthur	95p
☐ The Far Side of Destiny	Dore Mullen	£1.50
☐ The Southern Moon	Jane Parkhurst	£1.25
☐ Summerblood	Anne Rudeen	£1.25
☐ The Year Growing Ancient	Irene Hunter Steiner	£1.10

HAMLYN WHODUNNITS

☐ The Worm of Death	Nicholas Blake	95p
☐ The Judas Pair	Jonathan Gash	95p
☐ There Came Both Mist and Snow	Michael Innes	95p
☐ The Siamese Twin Mystery	Ellery Queen	95p

FICTION

HISTORICAL ROMANCE/ROMANCE/SAGA

☐ Flowers of Fire	Stephanie Blake	£1.00
☐ So Wicked My Desire	Stephanie Blake	£1.50
☐ Morgana	Marie Buchanan	£1.35
☐ The Enchanted Land	Jude Deveraux	£1.50
☐ Mystic Rose	Patricia Gallagher	£1.25
☐ Alinor	Roberta Gellis	£1.20
☐ Gilliane	Roberta Gellis	£1.00
☐ Joanna	Roberta Gellis	£1.25
☐ Roselynde	Roberta Gellis	£1.20
☐ Love's Scarlet Banner	Fiona Harrowe	£1.00
☐ Lily of the Sun	Sandra Heath	95p
☐ Daneclere	Pamela Hill	£1.25
☐ Strangers' Forest	Pamela Hill	£1.00
☐ Royal Mistress	Patricia Campbell Horton	£1.50
☐ The Tall One	Barbara Jefferis	£1.00
☐ Captive Bride	Johanna Lindsey	£1.00
☐ The Flight of the Dove	Catherine MacArthur	95p
☐ The Far Side of Destiny	Dore Mullen	£1.50
☐ The Southern Moon	Jane Parkhurst	£1.25
☐ Summerblood	Anne Rudeen	£1.25
☐ The Year Growing Ancient	Irene Hunter Steiner	£1.10

HORROR/OCCULT/NASTY

☐ The Howling	Gary Brandner	85p
☐ Return of the Howling	Gary Brandner	95p
☐ Dying Light	Evan Chandler	85p
☐ Curse	Daniel Farson	95p
☐ Trance	Joy Fielding	90p
☐ The Janissary	Alan Lloyd Gelb	95p
☐ Rattlers	Joseph L. Gilmore	85p
☐ Slither	John Halkin	95p
☐ Devil's Coach-Horse	Richard Lewis	85p
☐ Spiders	Richard Lewis	80p
☐ Poe Must Die	Marc Olden	£1.00
☐ The Spirit	Thomas Page	£1.00
☐ The Force	Alan Radnor	90p
☐ Bloodthirst	Mark Ronson	90p
☐ Ghoul	Mark Ronson	95p
☐ Ogre	Mark Ronson	95p
☐ Return of the Living Dead	John Russo	80p
☐ The Scourge	Nick Sharman	£1.00
☐ Deathbell	Guy N. Smith	95p
☐ The Specialist	Jasper Smith	85p

WESTERN BLADE SERIES

☐ No. 1 The Indian Incident	Matt Chisholm	75p
☐ No. 2 The Tucson Conspiracy	Matt Chisholm	75p
☐ No. 3 The Laredo Assignment	Matt Chisholm	75p

NAME ....

ADDRESS ....

....

Write to Hamlyn Paperbacks Cash Sales, PO Box 11, Falmouth, Cornwall TR10 9EN.

Please indicate order and enclose remittance to the value of the cover price plus:

U.K.: 30p for the first book, 15p for the second book and 12p for each additional book ordered to a maximum charge of £1.29.

B.F.P.O. & EIRE: 30p for the first book, 15p for the second book plus 12p per copy for the next 7 books, thereafter 6p per book.

OVERSEAS: 50p for the first book plus 15p per copy for each additional book.

Whilst every effort is made to keep prices low it is sometimes necessary to increase cover prices and also postage and packing rates at short notice. Hamlyn Paperbacks reserve the right to show new retail prices on covers which may differ from those previously advertised in the text or elsewhere.